Through the Eye of a Needle

Hal Clement

A Del Rey Book

BALLANTINE BOOKS • NEW YORK

A Del Rey Book
Published by Ballantine Books

Copyright © 1978 by Hal Clement

Map by Bob Porter

Library of Congress Catalog Card Number: 78-57488

ISBN 0-345-28410-0

Manufactured in the United States of America

First Edition: June 1978
Second Printing: February 1979
First Canadian Printing: July 1978

Cover art by H. R. Van Dongen

Dedicated to Scratch, for Needling

Contents

Apology		ix
1.	Generalities	1
2.	Details	16
3.	Complications	29
4.	Arrangements and People	46
5.	When in Doubt, Ask	61
6.	The Moral of a White Lie	74
7.	Joke	90
8.	Routine, Modified	104
9.	Joke Two	115
10.	Joke Three	128
11.	First Aid	142
12.	Joker	157
13.	Reconstruction	174
14.	Professional	185
15.	Official, from Headquarters	192

Apology

Everyone wants to make an impression on history, but most of us would prefer it to be a good impression. Some twenty-eight years ago, I wrote a story called NEEDLE, many of whose characters reappear in this book. In that story, I frequently referred to one or the other of the partners in the biological relation called *symbiosis* as a *symbiote*. It will be obvious to many that I was never exposed to a course in the classic tongues of Italy or Greece. A biology-teaching colleague pointed out to me, gently and courteously but much too late, that the proper word is *symbiont*.

Unfortunately, my erroneous contribution to the language has appeared quite frequently in other stories and even in their titles. I regret this, but don't know what I can do about it except what I am doing now. I formally withdraw the word *symbiote*, and in this book replace it with the proper one.

Those who still have hopes of formulating a science which will describe social phenomena will, I trust, have fun observing the results of this action.

If any.

Hal Clement

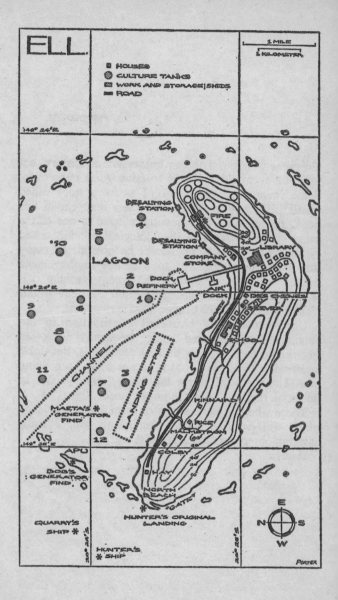

ELL.

- ⬛ HOUSES
- ⬤ CULTURE TANKS
- ▨ WORK AND STORAGE SHEDS
- ▬ ROAD

1 MILE

1 KILOMETER

145° 24' E.

DESALTING STATION

FIRE

DESALTING STATION

LIBRARY

5

10

LAGOON

COMPANY STORE

145° 2d' E.

2

DOCK
REFINERY

AIR

DOCK

DES CHENES

9

6

10

BREWER

8

SCHOOL

11

CHANNEL

7

3

LANDING STRIP

KINNAIRD

RICE

MAETA'S * GENERATOR FIND

MALMSTROM (60)

145° 28' E.

12

COLEY

APU

WAY

DOB'S GENERATOR FIND

NORTH BEACH

"GATE"

QUARRY'S SHIP *

HUNTER'S ORIGINAL LANDING

HUNTER'S * SHIP

E
N — S
W

PORTER

I. Generalities

Of the three people in the cockpit of the Catalina, one was slightly bored, one was extremely uncomfortable but too embarrassed to admit it, and the third was wondering whether he had done the right thing.

The pilot had made the trip from Tahiti to Ell often enough and had enough thousands of hours in the amphibian that little of his conscious attention was needed for either operation or navigation. The weather was bumpy but called for no special concern, and the aircraft itself was reliable enough to demand only the routine worries of the man's profession.

Robert Kinnaird did not regard the weather with the same indifference. He knew as well as the man in the other seat that there was no danger, but the knowledge didn't seem to help his nervous system at the reflex level. His eyes and his semicircular canals were feeding conflicting data to his brain. The Pacific was garnished with convection cells that afternoon; some of them were visible by virtue of the cumulus puffs which topped them, but others could only make themselves felt. The young man had several times been on the verge of suggesting that they climb above the cumulus tops, but he knew what the answer would be. Dulac, the pilot, had very professional ideas about fuel conservation, even on a short trip such as this. His combat-flying over the same ocean during the early forties had given him a clear idea of the magnitude of the water-to-land ratio even in areas where islands were frequent.

Kinnaird himself had insisted on making the flight

that afternoon, rather than early the following morning. Dulac had warned him that it would be a bumpy ride. All that Bob could do was feel irritated at the third member of the group, and he knew that any such annoyance was both unjustified and futile. He had known for years that the Hunter would do nothing about such a trivial phenomenon as motion sickness.

The Hunter himself was not quite sure whether he should take steps or not. The flight was, of course, Bob's own fault; there was no practical reason why they couldn't have waited until the next day. The human youth knew, from both precept and experience, that his alien companion would do everything in his power to preserve him from real injury or illness, but that he did not want to encourage Bob to lean at all heavily on the being's invisible presence. The four pounds of jelly distributed throughout the man's body cavities knew that total dependence on another being could lead to even more trouble than seven years of partial dependence already had. The Hunter, these days, tended to lean over backward to avoid doing anything more than basic scratch-plugging. He knew that he was overreacting, and that a little nerve pressure to ease his host's nausea would probably do no real harm; but with Bob's health at its present level, he could not bring himself to take a chance. After all, the trip couldn't take much longer.

In an attempt to be consoling, he pointed this out to Bob. The pilot could not hear him, since the sound of the Hunter's voice originated in his host's middle-ear bones, vibrated by threads of unhuman tissue; but the response was less well concealed.

"Don't tell me it won't be long!" snapped Kinnaird. "It's been three and a half eternities already, and the island isn't in sight yet. Why didn't you talk me out of it?" His voice was not quite audible, though he did speak—the Hunter was not a mind reader, though he could interpret the emotion behind most of Bob's involuntary muscular and glandular responses. The pilot might possibly have heard the mutter if the engines had not been running.

"What was I supposed to say?" retorted the Hunter. "I did point out that Dulac was right about the roughness of the flight. Since you have final say about any of our activities—unless I want to exercise veto by knocking you out—there was nothing much more I could do. You chose to face it—now face it. After all, there's nothing in your stomach to lose even if your control does go."

"I wish you'd exercise that veto right now. At least I'd be comfortable until we get down. I mean it, Hunter. I've never felt worse in my life. Maybe the other trouble is contributing, but I really don't think I can put up with it any longer."

The Hunter was tempted for a moment, but decided against taking the chance.

"This isn't that sort of emergency, and you know it," the alien said. "I'm sorry you're so uncomfortable, but no one ever dies of motion sickness, as your own people say. They—"

"If you say what I think you're about to, I'll get drunk the minute we get home!" Bob interrupted, almost loudly enough to attract Dulac's attention. The Hunter, whose main aim was to keep his host's attention from his own stomach, refrained from repeating the cliché, and simply changed the subject. The remark about alcohol he assumed—and hoped—was not meant seriously; Bob definitely knew better than to take chances with his symbiont's personal coordination.

"Do you really think we can get anywhere without letting more human beings know about me?" the alien asked. "We're going to need a lot of help."

"I'm hoping for most from Doc Seever," Bob replied. "His hours are kind of irregular, of course, since there's no way to predict sickness or injury there on the island, but he certainly knows more of what has to be known than anyone else there. Dad'll be too busy to help, most of the time. We really should have some people who are either a lot lower in the PFI chain of command and don't have much but eight-to-five responsibilities, or people who don't work for the outfit at all. The latter will be hard to find on Ell."

"Your mother is a competent person."

"She'll have to spend too much time looking after Silly."

"Your sister is six years old, now. She shouldn't need very much of your mother's time—won't she be in school by now?"

"Maybe. I've almost forgotten when school keeps, down here."

The discussion was interrupted by a tap on Bob's shoulder, felt by both speakers. Both looked ahead, the Hunter having no choice in the matter. The island which Bob regarded as home, though he had been away from it well over half the time for the last ten years, was clearly visible ahead, the low sun accenting the ridges which formed the two arms of the L-shape, and gleaming from the square outlines of the culture tanks which studded the lagoon. Dulac banked a trifle to the right, and eased back on the throttles.

"We'll be down in fifteen minutes," he assured his passenger.

"Good." Bob's approval was very sincere. "I'm sorry I talked you into a ride this bumpy, but at least we'll be home that much sooner."

"You mean you will. It doesn't matter that much to me where I sleep. What you've talked me into is having tomorrow off, thanks. I was supposed to get this bucket to Ell by tomorrow night for work the next day. As far as the ride was concerned, you did all the suffering, so don't apologize to me."

Bob had done a little flying during his college years, though nothing as large and heavy as the Dumbo had been involved. The procedures of letdown, pattern entry, and final approach were meaningful enough to keep his attention off his stomach for the remaining minutes of the flight. They swept above the western arm of the island, almost above Bob's home, at five hundred feet, though only the pilot could see the house—they were in a left bank onto the downwind leg, and when they leveled on an eastward heading, the land was behind and to their left.

Final approach carried the amphibian over the shorter leg of the L, only a few feet above its ridge and the tanks it carried. Bob thought he recognized a few faces on the long causeway which led out to the dock where the tankers loaded, but didn't have time to be sure. He had the impression that there were more houses in the village—the area at the bend of the L, where the road from the causeway met the one which ran the length of the island, but again he couldn't be sure; there were too many trees. It was likely enough that there were; Pacific Fuels, Incorporated, had been doing very well, especially during the recent Korean troubles, and the population of the island had been climbing. It had been about one hundred and seventy when the Hunter had first come ashore on Ell nearly eight years before, after his crash in the ocean outside the reef; now, both he and his host knew, it was about fifty greater. Many of the new ones were children, of course, but by no means all. The store, the school, and the library had all been enlarged, and more adults were needed to take care of the increased production facilities.

The landing area was marked off by buoys, and the numerous boats and canoes on the lagoon were safely clear. Dulac touched down within twenty yards of the runway's beginning, let the amphibian come to a near halt, and manipulated his throttles to bring the machine about. This brought the right cockpit seat, occupied by Bob and the Hunter, toward the shore, and both examined the island eagerly for changes; they had not been there for two years. Even from here, however, the trees kept them from seeing much. The long northwest leg of the island was still heavily jungled.

Boats could be examined more easily. Most of the

ones occupied by juveniles were now being paddled, rowed, or sailed toward the long dock, though their owners were careful to keep out of the airplane's way. The island population was of a mixed descent that was largely Polynesian, and the adults were casual about allowing children of all ages on and in the water, but took a very dim view of their offspring's violating the more common-sense safety rules of swimming and boat-handling. Few of the youngsters would have risked being kept ashore for a week or so, since they got no sympathy from their friends.

They even left tie-up room at the float, a twenty-yard-square structure two hundred yards from shore connected by a slanting gangway to the main dock. The raft itself was crowded with youngsters by the time the amphibian nosed into the notch provided for it, but they kept well back from the propellers as Dulac cut his mixtures and let the blades whirl to a stop. Bob and the Hunter knew most of the faces in the crowd, but were attracted to a lanky, six-foot-plus blond youth who approached with a line in his hands and began the job of mooring the aircraft. It was Kenneth Malmstrom, one of the quintet who had shared unknowingly in the Hunter's police problem seven years before.

The sight of the young worker sent their minds in two different directions as Bob and his symbiont made their way back toward the hatch of the Catalina. Kinnaird himself was wondering whether any of the others would be on the island. He knew that two of them, Hay and Colby, were at colleges in Melbourne and Arizona respectively; but Rice was working for PFI and might be around, and Bob had been seriously considering his help in the new problem.

The Hunter was not thinking that far ahead. He was wondering whether Malmstrom, obviously available, could be trusted with the information he would need to be really helpful. The alien was inclined to doubt it. Of the five, Malmstrom had always seemed to him the least mature and reliable. It might or might not be relevant that he had not taken up the standing company offer of a college education for any of the island children, in return for a six-year contract after graduation. Many young people refused for reasons quite unconnected with intelligence. Still, Malmstrom seemed content with a low-responsibility job which demanded little of his imagination and brains, and the Hunter hoped that Bob would not get too enthusiastic on the strength of meeting the first of his old friends after a two-year absence.

The enthusiasm was certainly there. The moment the taller youth saw Bob at the hatch, he dropped the line he was holding and sprang toward him.

"Bob! You old bookworm! Are you back for good?" He shook hands violently, and he and Bob went through the backslapping routine which still bothered the Hunter after more than seven years. He knew the injury involved was negligible, but several human lifetimes of habit are hard to break.

"I guess so," answered Kinnaird. "I haven't signed anything yet, but might as well get my degree worked off as soon as possible. You knew I was coming, didn't you?"

"Sure, but not just when. We really didn't expect Marc and his Dumbo until tomorrow. When you were sighted, they phoned me to get down here and earn my dividend. Maybe I ought to get a job in the States, where work hours are a lot more definite. Out here they expect things to be done whenever they have to be done, no matter what time it is—even dinner time."

"How do you like what you're doing?" asked Bob.

"What more's to ask for? I sweat a few hours each day, get paid for it, and do what I want the rest of the time."

The Hunter was not surprised by this answer, and hoped that his host would take it as evidence of Malmstrom's unsuitability for their project. Of course, there was no risk of premature disclosure with the present crowd around them—unless Bob collapsed—

but it was always possible that words might escape which would be hard to cover up later, unless Bob shared the Hunter's doubts about "Shorty."

In the hope of forestalling any such slip, the alien put a question of his own into Bob's ear.

"How about Rice? Is he here on Ell?" Kinnaird could have answered his symbiont without attracting attention, but there seemed no need this time. He simply repeated the question aloud.

"No, he's on Tahiti."

"Working for PFI, of course."

"Oh, sure. He gets over here every so often. I don't know just what he does, but it doesn't let him get outside much. I haven't seen anyone with lighter skin until you showed up. Doesn't the sun shine in the States any more?"

"Some places. New England uses other things in its tourist literature."

"Such as?"

"Oh, its brain factories." Malmstrom had finished mooring the aircraft, and was helping Dulac get its cargo onto the float. Bob had been removing his own luggage at the same time, doing his best to keep his physical condition from being too obvious. He did not succeed very well; both he and the Hunter were disturbed at Malmstrom's next remark.

"They don't make muscles there, do they? You're pretty far out of shape, Bob old buddy."

Kinnaird gave a shrug, covering as well as he could. "It's been quite a trip. I'll take you on in a few days, after I get rested up."

The conversation was interrupted, to the relief of the Hunter and his host, by a shrill voice from the main causeway above.

"Bob! What did you bring me?"

The sun was just on the horizon, in Bob's eyes as he looked toward the dock, but he didn't need to see to identify the speaker. Daphne, his six-year-old sister, was plunging down the gangway at a rate which made the Hunter uneasy, even though he had no direct responsibility for the small creature's well-being. He remarked to his host, "If she had been around when I first met you, I'd have been led badly astray in our little problem."

Bob chuckled, knowing what his symbiont meant. The Hunter had been seeking a fugitive of his own species who had escaped into space. Pursued and pursuer had crashed near Ell; both had made their ways ashore and found human hosts. The Hunter had been faced with the task of locating the other without help from his fellow police, without a background situation in which everybody harbored a symbiont of his own and took for granted that everyone else did, and without any of the technical equipment which would normally have helped him to locate his quarry and separate it from its host without harm to the latter. He had succeeded because the criminal had made no effort to train his host in elementary personal care. The symbionts were able to stop bleeding from injuries, to dispose of infecting microorganisms, and within limits even to minimize pain. Human beings, like the humanoid species of the Hunter's home planet, tend to limit their behavior by what they find themselves getting away with; if sixty miles an hour doesn't hurt them, they are soon doing sixty-five.

Arthur Kinnaird, Bob's father, by all accounts a normally cautious adult of his species, had become increasingly casual about situations offering personal danger. He had been getting away with everyday actions which should have given him cuts, sprains, bruises, splinters, even minor burns; he had expanded his behavior accordingly . . .

That had been seven and a half Earth years ago. Now Arthur's daughter was acting as though nothing on the planet could hurt *her*. The Hunter might have wondered whether his old quarry had survived after all, but Daphne had been the same at the age of four; the Hunter did not criticize to Bob, but he felt that either her parents or her culture or both were taking better care of her than was strictly healthy.

Whether he liked it or not, it was not his problem. He had made enough mistakes of his own, with his own host, and would have to solve the problems those had created, first.

If he could.

Daphne swarmed up her brother, squirrel fashion, chattering. She was genuinely glad to see him; the question of what he had brought for her was not repeated. Bob, to the Hunter's relief, was able to support the forty pounds or so of her rather skinny form, but both symbiont and host were relieved when she dropped back to the float and took up a wild dance around him.

"Should I drop you overboard to cool you off, Silly?" her brother asked.

"Go ahead. Mother wouldn't let me swim out, but if you do I'll just swim in."

Bob made no attempt to continue the argument. He captured the child, more or less immobilized her, and greeted his mother, who had descended the gangway more sedately.

"Hi, Mom. You're here pretty quickly. Were you waiting for me?"

"Just hoping. We heard the plane and biked down on the chance. I hope someone took pictures of your graduation; I wish we could have gone."

"I have 'em. You're letting this monkey use a bike already? I'm surprised she didn't ride it down the plank."

Daphne assumed an indignant expression, barely visible in the swiftly gathering darkness. "Of course not," she said. "I'm not allowed to ride the bike on the dock."

"Good for you, Mom. I never thought rules would take with this one."

"She's no worse than you were," his mother pointed out. "Locking up the bike a couple of times made her see reason. As I recall, with you and that deathtrap of a boat your friends had at first—"

"All right. We were all young once."

"Good Heavens. You really *have* been to college, haven't you? Come on home, you must be hungry. Grab what's most important of your stuff. We can help. If you did bring your sister anything, tell us what it's in and we'll take it with us whatever it weighs. Discipline is one thing, but making her wait until your father can jeep everything up to the house would be a bit cruel."

"Credit me with some sense. The whatever-it-is is in the light suitcase. She can carry it up by herself if she's feeling strong and ambitious."

"Open it up and give it to me here, and carry the rest of the bag yourself," was the girl's prompt suggestion.

"Not until your big, strong brother has had a good meal and some rest. That's the deal; take it or leave it."

Bob was still covering fairly well, but both he and the Hunter knew that it couldn't be managed much longer. They had agreed from the first that the older Kinnairds would have to be given all the details, but they were almost as sure that the child should not. Also, Malmstrom, Dulac, and much of Ell's juvenile population were still there at the float. Bob simply *had* to last a while longer.

Malmstrom had heard the last part of the conversation. "I'll help right now if you like, Bob," he cut in. "We can get the heavy stuff up to the dock, and then you or your dad or whoever can come by with a jeep and run it up to your house." Bob and the Hunter wondered for a moment how they could get out of that one, even as they absorbed the implication that powered vehicles were as hard to get, and as commonly owned, on the island as they used to be. Before either of them could think of an excuse, Bob's mother saved the situation.

"Thanks, Ken, but I'd rather he didn't take the time now. I know we'll be seeing a lot of him from now on, but it's been nearly two years since we have. I'd like to get him home, feed him, and talk to him.

Let me play old-fashioned mother just this once. If you see my husband, tell him I'd rather he came right home without bothering about the luggage tonight."

"Sure, Mrs. Kinnaird. I'll help with this stuff any time they don't have me doing something else. I suppose some of it goes to the library, anyway."

"Those two big ones," Bob pointed out.

"Did you really have to read all that? Glad I made the choice I did. I'll see you around, Bob; any idea what they'll have you doing?"

"Well, I have a degree with high honors in chemical engineering from one of the most prestigious institutions east of the Hudson River, so they'll probably want to show me that there are eight experienced chemical engineers on Ell already and that my muscles will be more useful to PFI than my brains for the next few years. We may be sweating side by side, for a while anyhow."

"I can believe it." Malmstrom waved farewell as the family group started up the gangway, and turned back to his work.

Bob had uttered not a serious prophecy but rather his and the Hunter's major worry. It was quite likely that he would be assigned to the less pleasant and more physical aspects of his long-term job, and in his present condition he wouldn't last out the first day. Stage One of the complex plan they had been working out involved getting the help of the island doctor to forestall such an assignment. Seever was one of the few people who knew about the Hunter, and the alien and his host were counting heavily on both his sympathy and his professional knowledge in what was to come.

The airplane float lay a quarter of a mile from shore along the causeway, and by the time the three walkers reached the inner end of the latter, darkness had fallen, though a gibbous moon made walking easy. With a sigh of relief, Daphne set down the suitcase she had been carrying.

"I can't take this on my bike," she pointed out. "You

take it on yours, Mom, and I'll walk mine home with Bob."

"You didn't bring mine?" asked her brother.

"How could we? We were riding our own."

"I'm glad there are still things I can teach you. Not right now, though; I'm kind of tired, and don't feel like walking all the way home." His mother looked anxious for a moment, but neither Bob nor the Hunter caught the expression.

"You've been going a good many hours," she said. "I don't blame you. Daph, leave the bag here and go look for your father—yes, on your bike, as long as you stay with the streetlights. He's somewhere down at this end. Have him get a jeep and meet us here." The child obeyed without a word, her mother smiling after her.

"She's not usually allowed to ride alone after dark. You've probably noticed the new lights—they're just here in the village, and go along the road only as far as the school, our way. How's the Hunter, son?"

Bob had no chance to answer. They were under one of the lights, at the point where the dock road met the one which ran the length of the island, and people had seen them. All of them knew Bob, and the island population—the older ones, this time—rapidly gathered to welcome him back and ask about his college life. The Hunter was completely uninterested in the conversation, quite worried about his host's chances of remaining on his feet long enough to reach his home, and annoyed at his own feeling of helplessness.

Eventually a jeep whipped down the road from the northwest and pulled to a stop beside the group. Bob's father and sister emerged, the latter ducking behind her mother without making any effort to recover the bicycle in the vehicle's back seat. Arthur Kinnaird, rather brusquely but without actual rudeness, broke up the gathering.

"Evening, Ben—Hi, Maria—Hello, everyone—Bob, hop in. We'll go out and get your stuff. Small fry, get your bike and go home with your mother. We'll be there as soon as you are. Sorry to take him away, folks, but he's been traveling long enough to need sleep. We won't even talk to him ourselves until tomorrow."

"I don't think he's right about that," the Hunter remarked to Bob as they started out the causeway. "You're not going to be able to carry luggage, and that's going to have to be explained to your father, at least."

But at first it seemed that no immediate explanation would be necessary, and the Hunter began to hope. Arthur Kinnaird insisted on his son's staying in the jeep while he made two trips down to the float. If Bob had been paying close attention to what he brought up, the explanation might have been put off until the next day: he did not need the footlocker that remained on the float, and if they had driven straight home after his father's first two trips, Bob would have had just enough strength to get inside the house. But his father made a third trip down to the float. He found, besides the footlocker, only the book crates which were obviously too large to attempt. He put his hand into one of the straps at the end, and gave an exclamation of pain. "Bob! Bring the flashlight down here, will you?"

The trip down the plank had to be made carefully, but Bob was still on his feet when they reached the bottom.

"What's the matter, Dad?" he asked. The elder Kinnaird removed his hand from his mouth long enough to answer.

"Cut myself on something under that locker handle. Take a look, will you?" He bent over to look himself as his son directed the flashlight beam to the indicated spot. The source of the cut was obvious enough.

"I didn't think we had anyone like that on the island," Arthur Kinnaird remarked. "Could it have happened anywhere else along the way?" The lid of the thin metal box had been pried roughly outward, and the stretched part of its edge had torn to form a jagged

V-shaped notch, its two corners projecting just above the loop of leather which formed the handle.

"I'm not a professional baggage thief, but that seems a silly way to go about it," replied his son. "You'd think anyone wanting to get at the contents would work on the latch or the hinges."

"What's in it?"

"Don't remember exactly, but nothing extra valuable. Mostly clothes, maybe some of the books for the library, though they're mostly in the big cases. I'd have to check to be sure. I accumulated a lot of junk while I was away, and I couldn't bear to throw much of it out, with PFI paying the freight home. Are you hurt much?"

"I'll live. Too bad you hadn't been working on carrying the footlocker. I suppose your friendly lump of green jelly is still with you—sorry I didn't say hello to you, Hunter, but you aren't that obvious."

"Yes, he's here still. If your cut's bad enough, we can—"

"It's not that serious. We can leave this thing here for now, since you don't think it has anything important. Let's try to get home before the ladies."

Bob hesitated; he was very near the limit.

"I'm not sure I can get myself up the gangway again," he admitted at last, knowing that now he could not put off explaining his weakness.

"Hmph. Your sister said you looked bushed. Was the trip that bad?"

"Even Silly noticed it? We were hoping she wouldn't. No, it wasn't the trip. It's more complicated, and I'm sure we're going to have to get Doc Seever in on it."

"You've been hurt? Something the Hunter couldn't fix, or hasn't had time to fix?"

"Not hurt. There hasn't been any accident. It's been coming on for a long time. I'll tell you and Mom about it after Silly's in bed; it'd be too much trying to make her understand—or have you told her about the Hunter?"

"Decidedly not. Come on, let's get you back to the

car. Do you mean you have some kind of disease that the Hunter can't handle?"

"On the contrary, you might say. Sorry to put it so bluntly, little friend, but—Dad, the Hunter has caused the trouble. What he or we or anyone can do is a wide-open question."

No more words were spoken the rest of the way up the plank.

2. Details

In spite of what had happened at the dock, the jeep reached the Kinnaird home very shortly behind the bicycles. The few minutes' rest as they drove restored Bob enough to let him get into the house without assistance, though the luggage stayed in the car for the moment.

The suitcase Daphne had carried was of course inside; her mother had yielded to the pressure, and carried it home on her own bicycle. The child promptly dragged it over to the couch on which her brother had thankfully collapsed.

She wanted it opened at once, of course, and the resulting activities filled the time until food was served. Every minute of rest that Bob could get was good, of course, and it was fortunate that Daphne was content to let him stay on the couch and hand out presents—very much plural, to the little girl's delight—which made up most of the contents of the suitcase.

The Hunter was getting quite impatient by the time she was sent to bed. Mrs. Kinnaird was perfectly aware that something was wrong by this time, though her husband had spoken only a word or two to her after his arrival; she, too, wanted to hear the details. Eventually, protesting but not really resentful, Daphne was dismissed upstairs to what had formerly been her brother's room. Fortunately, since he could certainly not have handled stairs too many times a day, Bob was to sleep in a wing which his father had built at the back of the house during the past year—largely a matter of luck, since he certainly had not foreseen his son's troubles.

Eventually the child was quiet, and the rest of the family was able to get down to business. Bob had long ago planned what he should say. The Hunter knew that he wouldn't enjoy listening, since the words could not possibly make him look very good, but was mature enough to face the situation.

It was the mother who opened the conversation, after a final trip upstairs to make sure the child was asleep.

"You're not just tired, are you, Bob? There's something more serious."

"I'm afraid so, Mom," was the answer. "I don't know just how serious—it might drag on for a long time, but it wouldn't be very smart to count on that. This actually started before I was home two years ago. It wasn't very bad then, and it didn't seem a good idea to worry either you or Doc Seever with it, but it's been getting worse ever since, and something really has to be done now."

"Does the Hunter have a reliable prognosis? I mean, has he encountered this sort of thing before?" Bob's father cut in.

"Not personally, he says. He's heard about it historically, when his species meets a new type of host. It wouldn't have happened now if he were a doctor instead of a detective. Let me give it to you from the beginning." Both his parents nodded their approval.

"You both know what the Hunter and his people are like—about four pounds of something vaguely like human protoplasm, but made of molecule-sized units instead of the relatively huge cells of our tissue.

His people can live independently, at least on their own planet, but normally exist inside the body of a larger creature in a state of symbiosis. The Hunter has been doing that with me for years, sharing the food I eat, seeing through my eyes, hearing with my ears, and paying for his keep by destroying invading germs, stopping blood loss from cuts, and so on. Also, he's a personal friend, though not as close as we might be on his home world; we don't have the facilities here which would let him live a normal life, and we don't have very similar interests. He's a detective, and his partner at home was also a police official; he went through my chemical and other courses in college with me, but didn't enjoy them as much as I did. On his world, partners don't join up until they've known each other for a long time. Here, he didn't have much choice.

"His people have had contact, since they've developed space travel, with other more or less humanlike races, and have been able to carry on the same sort of life-sharing with these. It's not so routine, though. No two planets, as far as their experience goes, seem to produce life with identical chemistry, and a lot has to be learned before the symbiosis really goes smoothly.

"Naturally, the Hunter's partnership with me is in the less well organized category. He was never completely sure that he wouldn't do me some harm. We're enough like the other humanoids he's known so that he could recognize and offset my normal immunity reactions in about the same way he was used to, and of course with him there I didn't need them—he could take care of infections. Just the same, he would check every few days to make sure his neutralization of my immune response to *him* hadn't had more general effects. For example, if I got a splinter in my finger he'd wait to make sure my body reacted normally before he cleaned up the intruding bacteria.

"A couple of years ago, I failed one of those tests. I got badly infected from a minor scratch, and the

Hunter found that my immunity chemistry just wasn't working at all any more. He took its place, of course; there was no danger as long as he was with me. Of course, if anything were to happen to him—" Bob didn't finish, but his parents nodded.

They remembered the circumstances which had caused them to learn about the Hunter—Seever, the island doctor, had been the only one Bob had let into the secret before the police project had been concluded. Bob had bluffed the alien fugitive into leaving his father's body, and destroyed the creature by fire; but the departure had been very hasty. A short time later, Arthur Kinnaird had fallen ill. The symptoms were a blend of pneumonia and meningitis, and Seever had been mystified. Eventually, he and Bob had persuaded the reluctant Hunter to transfer to Arthur Kinnaird's body to investigate.

The problem had proven straightforward enough; viruslike cells left behind by the fugitive in its hasty departure had lost the control and coordination of an intelligent creature, and were simply living without regard for the welfare of their host—the sort of thing, on a much cruder level, which the organism originating them had done and which had made it a criminal by the standards of its species.

The Hunter had had no trouble incorporating the units into his own structure. Seever had felt it necessary to give the whole story to Bob's mother, who was quite intelligent enough to recognize and be bothered by any half-truths; and later on, when her husband had regained his senses, he had also been told. Under the circumstances they had little choice about believing, and had eventually come to take the Hunter for granted—even addressing him directly at times, though of course their son had to transmit any answers.

"In a way," Bob went on, "I'm a sort of addict of my symbiont. It's not just the immunity thing, now. Other parts of my personal chemistry keep going haywire every few months. Sometimes the Hunter can spot the actual cause and do something about it, sometimes he has to use his own abilities in a way not really related to my own body's handling of the same problem—for example, the way he handles infection by consuming the organisms responsible instead of chemical neutralization.

"He's described the whole thing as a juggling act. As time goes on, he has to devote more and more effort and attention to keeping my machinery going. Quite often some step he takes interferes with one or more of the things that he's already doing, or that my own biochemistry is normally doing. Unless we can find some fairly simple key *cause* for all this and do something effective about it—well, he admits that sooner or later the juggler is bound to drop a plate."

"I suppose he can't just withdraw entirely and let nature take care of the situation," Mrs. Kinnaird asked.

"Nature isn't that interested in me," her son replied. "The juggling act is just what every living body goes into, and drops out of, sooner or later. Letting things go on their own and shutting eyes and ears may produce 'natural' results, but there's no way to be sure your own survival is included in the meaning of 'natural.' Knowledge is what is needed if you hope for things to go your way."

"But surely the Hunter has the knowledge! You told us he could identify thousands, maybe millions, of chemicals—even unbelievably complex things like proteins—by his own senses. He can produce lots of them deliberately. You once said that if you got diabetes he could take over the making of insulin for you."

"I did, I do, and he does. He can do a lot. He *is* doing a lot, but he has his limits, and they're a long way short of complete takeover of the chemical machinery of a human body. What you miss is the fact that, unbelievable as his abilities are, the complexity of the problem is even more unbelievable. You're more realistic than the weirdos who think you can heal a burn by shining the proper color of light on it, but you're still not really in touch with the problem."

"Then this weakness of yours is a continuing thing?" Bob's father asked.

"Not exactly—that is, I'm not weak and tired all the time. One of the plates that's slipping has something to do with my muscles. The Hunter can't spot anything specifically wrong with them, or with their individual cells, or with the way the cells are interacting and using food, or with the nerves connected with them; but after I've started to get tired—only a little tired, or what should make me only a little tired, they just lose power. The Hunter not only can't sense the cause, he can't even provide a makeshift remedy like delivering sugar or other necessities to the cells directly—it doesn't work. It isn't a matter of getting more fuel to the cells, or running stronger messages along the nerves, or a lot of other things—he could tell us thousands of things it isn't."

There was silence for many minutes.

The older people could not, of course, believe that there was no solution to the problem. This was their child. No longer really a child, and not even their only one, but theirs. They had taken for granted that he would still be alive when their own jugglers dropped the last plate. They would have been embarrassed to say aloud that there *had* to be an answer, but neither could think along any other line.

Neither thought consciously of blaming the Hunter for what had happened, though the wife thought fleetingly that it would have been nice if the alien had chosen to take up existence with the doctor after completion of his police project—Seever might have been able to take effective steps while the problem was still simple. She never brought this point up aloud, however. It was she who finally broke the silence.

"What do you and the Hunter plan to do, now that you're here?" she asked. "You must have a plan—you'd be looking even worse than you do, without one."

"Do you really think Ben Seever can do anything?" was Arthur Kinnaird's contribution. "He can't possibly know as much as the Hunter, even if he is a doctor rather than a detective."

Bob nodded basic agreement with the point; it was one he and the Hunter had considered long before.

"I don't know what he can do, Dad, but we can't help being better off with him than without him. We're telling him the whole story tomorrow. I'd have to see him anyway, since I'll be expected to have a checkup before reporting to work; tomorrow's Friday, and I'm sure PFI will expect my muscles to be available Monday. If nothing else, Doc may be able to think of something which will keep me out of heavy muscle work. If I don't do anything useful at all, they'll want to send me to the States or Japan for a real medical going-over, and we've got to stay here."

"Why?" both parents asked at once. Bob smiled.

"Don't give up when you first hear it. The basic assumption may be wrong, but at least it's not ridiculous. Our first job is to find one or both of the ships that crashed near Ell nearly eight years ago. What do you know about self-contained diving gear, Dad?"

Arthur Kinnaird, quite predictably, ignored the question and put one of his own.

"What good will the ships do? Are there supposed to be medical supplies in them? Would anything useful have lasted this long under water?"

"Probably not," admitted Bob. "We're not looking for supplies or equipment. The Hunter's ship was certainly thoroughly wrecked, and it's likely the other one was too. We need something else.

"We—the Hunter and I—have been thinking this through for over two years now, and we've reached one very firm conclusion. This problem can be solved, if at all, only by specialists among the Hunter's own races. This sort of thing has happened to them before when they encountered new species, and at least some of the time they have found answers."

Arthur Kinnaird was frowning thoughtfully; his

wife's expression was more hopeful. The man spoke first.

"How on Earth, if the phrase means anything, will finding either of those ships get you in touch with specialists from the Hunter's world? Do you think there are radios in them that will reach that far? And did you ever figure out where he came from, anyway? I thought he said he was hopelessly lost among the stars."

"Let's see, Dad; in order, if I can. No, neither of us expects to find anything usable in either ship. Radios wouldn't mean anything even if they worked; it would take fifty years or so for electromagnetic waves to make the trip one way. Our idea is a little less direct and maybe a little less promising, but we think it's more than just wishing.

"It's true that when I first knew him, and for quite a while afterward, the Hunter believed he was hopelessly lost. It wasn't until I took an astronomy course, with him looking on of course, that he got a reasonable idea of how thinly the stars are scattered in space, and how few are the possibilities that would have to be considered by the people who might be looking for him. He knows the time he traveled, though not the distance in any of our units. His departure direction was known to his own people, though of course they won't know how far he went. He feels sure that when he failed to return in a few of our months, searchers would have followed his line. He is even more sure that he did not pass at all close to any stars likely to distract those searchers; ours was the first that he and his quarry came at all close to. His friends should have had no trouble in finding this planetary system."

"But there are nine planets going around our sun," Mrs. Kinnaird pointed out, "and even if they narrowed it down to this one there are a lot of square miles to cover."

"That's why—or one reason why—we need to find the ships. They'll help us estimate the searchers' chance of narrowing down. The Hunter says that even when they're shut down, the faster-than-light engines involve force fields which can be spotted from millions of miles away—that's how he was able to follow the other ship. He's not sure how long the fields would last, or how far away they can be sensed, after the sort of violence which his own ship suffered. Sooner or later corrosion would destroy them so completely that no field effects would remain, and that's another reason we want to find them—to see how far that process may have gone."

"But no matter what their condition, what can you and the Hunter, or the rest of us, do about it?" asked his father.

"It will affect our plans. If the ships were detectable, searchers will have already covered this island very thoroughly—probably when the Hunter and I weren't here. If they weren't, at least the searchers would have found Earth, and the Hunter is certain they'd have been interested in the planet and in humanity. They'd have gone home, reported, and by now a team would be somewhere on the planet giving it a going-over for five to ten years to decide whether they should make open contact with humanity. If I could be sure of living ten years, we could sit back and wait."

"Assuming they decided in favor," his mother pointed out.

"Yes—I suppose I shouldn't be taking that for granted. In any case, we can't wait. The real question we have to solve is whether there'd be members of the Hunter's species here on Ell, as there would be if they'd found the ships, or whether all of Earth has to be searched. I must admit I'm hoping for the first."

"But would they be still here if they had found them?"

"Not steadily, but they'd come back from time to time to check on the pilots. They'd have found no trace of them, and they'd want to rescue the Hunter and arrest the other one."

"Why should they care about the arrest, after such a long time?" the woman asked. "Was he that terrible a criminal?"

"I don't know—just a minute." Bob waited while the Hunter covered the point, then relayed.

"He had done things for his own convenience which endangered his host, without the latter's consent. He was therefore self-centered enough to be a danger to any human beings he used; they'd want to get him as a protection to our own people."

"Would he have done what the Hunter has done to you?" asked his father. It was the first time he had let bitterness enter the conversation.

"That's not fair, Dad. The Hunter didn't do this on purpose, and he's trying to repair the trouble. The other one would simply have found himself another host when I became too messed up to be useful— probably long before now, since it's taking a lot of effort to keep me going already."

"All right. Sorry. Why wouldn't these searchers have left messages around for the Hunter?"

"Because they couldn't be sure the other one had been disposed of, of course. For the next obvious question with a less obvious answer, where would the Hunter leave messages for the searchers—except in the ships? It would have to be someplace they'd examine closely, and they won't check every drain pipe on this island, much less on Earth. Anything which could be seen from any distance would attract human attention, which would be very bad until the team decides about open contact."

"And if they haven't found the ships?"

"Then neither of us has any good ideas. The best is to publish some of the Hunter's police codes, transcribed as closely into local alphabets as possible, in large-circulation papers; but that's not very promising with, say, fifty investigators scattered over the planet. We'll try that if we have to—it'll take even more help than the other operation—but we certainly hope we don't have to."

"So do I." Arthur Kinnaird's voice had dropped from its earlier rather sharp intensity. "All right. You've made your case for doing some diving. We'd better find out whether those mine detectors they used in the war will work under water—"

"In principle, yes," Bob interrupted. "We'd have to make sure water didn't get into their circuitry, though. Do you think we can get hold of one? It should make a big difference, especially if the ships are under coral or mud by now."

"We'll try. There's nothing else we can do. I wish I could be more optimistic. Hunter, when you come right down to it, you really can't be sure whether any of your people have reached or will reach Earth, can you?"

The alien relayed a "No" through his young host, very reluctantly. He had problems enough without destroying Bob's morale, he felt. However, the word seemed to make no difference to the young chemist. Certainly his father noticed nothing, and was not thinking along such lines, for he went on,

"Is it really possible you can feel sure they can find this solar system? I can see their picking out Earth if they do, but photos I've seen of the Milky Way star clouds look pretty discouraging when it comes to a hide-and-seek game. Bob, look at the ceiling and start reading the Hunter's answer to that. I don't want to discourage anyone—I don't want to be discouraged myself, but I've got to have a realistic idea."

"He doesn't talk to me by shadowing the retinas any more, Dad; he speaks directly into my ear bones. But I'll relay."

The Hunter couldn't afford to hesitate, under the circumstances. He spoke, and his host quoted.

"The only doubt is raised by the nature of your sun, which is much brighter and hotter than ours. It is possible that there are stars more like our own which lay fairly close to our line of flight; I can only say that my instruments failed to detect them. If they got a really good fix on our departure direction, which they should have very easily, they would have to examine this system. It is possible they'll have to check others, too, but I've been here for nearly eight of your years. I honestly consider the chances very good indeed that some of my species are on Earth right now."

"There was no chance of his dodging?"

"He was an even less experienced astronaut than I. If he ever wanted to get back home, he would not have dodged."

"Would he have wanted to get back? What was he running from? Enough to make him panic?"

"Nothing capital. He would have been sentenced to ten or fifteen of your years in symbiosis with an unintelligent work animal—a hard labor sentence."

"And how long is that to your people, subjectively? How long do you normally live?"

The Hunter had never expected that question, and was totally unprepared to dodge it. He had never intended to discuss the matter with any human being, least of all with his own host. However, the questioner was waiting for an answer, and any sort of hesitation would do more harm than good.

"Our own life spans are rather indefinite, though we do die eventually. The beings we originally learned to live with, on my home world, usually last about forty of your years with our help. We average perhaps a dozen times that, but cannot count on it. The sentence, if anything, would have seemed milder to him than to you. In any case, we are now guessing about what other people would be guessing. I must admit that there is no absolute certainty that my people have come or will come to this planet, but I consider the chances good enough to justify planning on that basis, especially when such a relatively short distance seems to be involved."

"Short distance? Then you think you've identified your home star?" Mrs. Kinnaird's voice was eager.

"We think so." Bob was speaking on his own, now. "It's a very funny group of stars, and only one system like it was ever mentioned in my astronomy course. We think it must be Castor. That's a six-star system —two bright ones very much like Sirius, each with a faint companion which we don't know much about because we can't see it—they just cause a periodic Doppler shift in the bright stars' spectra—and finally a pair of red dwarf suns circling the others a long way out. We know a lot about those because they form an eclipsing spectroscopic pair; we think they must be the suns for the Hunter's planet, because everything we could check about brightness and periods and so on seemed to fit. They're what are called flare stars, which fits, too. The whole thing is forty-five or fifty light-years away. The Hunter isn't really sure about the speeds of their interstellar flyers, but thinks the distance is reasonable."

"You've mixed a few pronouns up—mostly the 'we's'—" his mother said, "but I think we get the picture. All right, we'll be optimistic too—we have to be, just as both of you do." The Hunter appreciated her choice of words; after the confession about his life span, it would not have been unreasonable for a human being to suspect that Bob was just another incident in his life, who would be dying a little sooner than his other hosts. In fact, the alien was seriously disturbed by Bob's situation, and at least as much bothered by his own responsibility for it. He was not permitting himself to think about his own future if they failed to save Bob's life.

Bob's father might have been as aware of this as his wife seemed to be, but his words provided no evidence either way. His job with PFI involved enough responsibility to make him a forceful and decisive person, and his words, after a few moments' thought, concerned only the actions to be taken.

"All right. Step one, Bob gets a good night's sleep so he can at least start tomorrow looking and acting normal. Two, he visits Ben Seever first thing in the morning, tells him everything, and takes whatever steps possible to get an assignment which won't make his condition any worse. It would be nice if it left him free for work on the search project, but we'll stay with possibles for the moment.

"Three, I do what I can about getting hold of free-diving equipment—I know there isn't any on Ell, but I think the company is experimenting with it on Tahiti. I also do research on metal-detecting equipment, its availability and usefulness for underwater work.

"The Hunter thinks of every possible way to get the attention of any of his people who may be on the island, or on Earth, without going to the extreme of publishing the whole story worldwide. I wouldn't mind doing that myself, but if it would interfere with whatever they'd normally be doing here, it might cause them to give up Earth as a bad job and leave. I don't see that that is really likely, but we're not taking the chance.

"Finally, both Bob and the Hunter give serious thought to which, and how many, additional people we might let into the business. I doubt that five people, one in shaky health and one restricted in his physical movements, are going to be enough. I know it will take thinking, but *think*."

But it was not thought which started the first recruiting action.

3. Complications

"Lighted any more fires lately?"

It was not a standard greeting by any criteria, and to both Bob and the Hunter it was more than disconcerting. The young woman who had given it was not herself surprising; they both had known Jenny Seever for years, and had heard that she was working for her father. As the island population had grown, the company had made additions to the Seever residence, turning it into a small hospital. Seever himself had had to become a little more formal in the matter of keeping records on his patients. The first thought to cross the minds of the two visitors was that Seever had made a record of the earlier project, and his daughter had come across it in the course of her work.

Bob, however, rejected this after a moment's thought. The doctor would not have written anything down, much less left the record where anyone else could find it, without first consulting Bob himself and his symbiont.

Nevertheless, the girl seemed to know something. The police project had indeed ended in a fire, an oil-fed bonfire which had consumed the alien fugitive, and the question could hardly be coincidence. However, Bob had read his share of detective stories, and was not going to be tricked into telling her more than she might already have learned.

"Lots," he answered, after a hesitation which he realized was probably revealing. "It was a good spring in the Northeast, and picnics were quite the thing before finals. Why?"

Jenny made no direct answer; her listeners got the impression that she had not expected the sort of response Bob had given. In this they were quite right. Since she was much quicker-witted than Bob or the Hunter, she knew better than to continue firing blindly after the first shot had missed. She changed the subject, letting the others make what they could of it— not that she thought of the man standing in front of her desk as representing two people, of course.

"I suppose you want to see Dad."

"Sure. I can't start work for PFI without a checkup, and I owe PFI several years of work in return for my chem degree, so obviously PFI wants me to have a checkup. Also, I'd like to see him anyway, just as an old friend. Is anyone with him now?"

"Yes. You'll have to wait." She couldn't resist one more shot. "Would you like some matches?"

"No, thanks. I don't smoke."

"Not even fuel oil?"

"Not for fun." The Hunter rather wished he could take part in the duel, but had to admit to himself that his host was doing well enough. Obviously the girl knew something; any chance of coincidence had vanished with the second question. It would be necessary to learn her status from the doctor before anything revealing could be said, but this seemed as obvious to Bob as it was to his symbiont.

"People have queer ideas of fun," Jenny countered.

"I see. Like being mysterious. Look, Kid, or Miss Seever, or whatever you want me to call you, I don't know what you're talking about." The Hunter, with the passion for strict truthfulness which had developed naturally in his long life, was rather disturbed by this remark. Even the reflection that it was not totally false, since Bob could really only guess what she was talking about, did not console him completely. "If someone has burned a house or something like that here on Ell, I don't know anything about it—I've been away for two years, and just got back last night. If you're talking about something else, you'll have to be specific enough to make sense. If you're just being funny, it isn't. If you've been reading mystery stories, change detectives. I'm not falling for the all-is-lost-fly-at-once line."

"Why should you?" she asked. Bob felt for a moment that he had made a slip, but carried on without a break that anyone but the Hunter could have spotted, both hoped.

"I shouldn't and I couldn't. There's nothing to fall for. If you're suggesting that I'm a pyromaniac, check your dad's files—you keep 'em now, don't you?"

"Thanks. That's an idea I hadn't thought of," she returned. "I'll do that when I have the time."

Neither spoke again for ten minutes or more. Bob sat, thinking of all the things he might have said differently. The Hunter made a few suggestions to him, but got no response. Jenny paid no obvious attention to her visible guest, and appeared to be busy with her normal paper work.

Eventually a door opened and a ten-year-old boy with his arm in a sling came through, followed by the doctor. The latter interrupted an admonishment about tree-climbing as he caught sight of Bob, came over to shake hands warmly, and ushered him into the examination room.

"Heard you were back—I suppose everyone has, by now. For good this time, isn't it? Did you drop over to be sociable, or are they putting you right to work? How are you, Hunter?—I suppose you're still there."

The Hunter almost answered; Seever was the one human being who sometimes made him forget that communication had to be by relay—who habitually spoke to him as though direct conversation were possible. Bob was usually amused by this, but showed no sign of it this time.

"Both, I guess," he answered Seever's last question first. "Yes, the Hunter is here. Nothing's been said officially to me about showing up for work, but I imagine they're taking it for granted. Unless I'm told otherwise, I'll be over at the main shop on Monday; but there are problems I'll need your help with, first."

"Oh?"

Bob wasted no time in recounting the situation; Seever listened silently. He nodded or raised an eyebrow at times, but said nothing until Bob had finished. Then he summarized.

"As I see it, you two want to find one or both of those spaceships, or their remains, as a step toward getting in touch with some of the Hunter's people who may or may not be on Earth, in the hope that they can solve, or get hold of someone else who can solve, Bob's medical difficulties, assuming they can be solved. Pretty iffy. We are hoping they can be, that they're actually on Earth, and that finding the ships will help you find the people. I won't ask pardon for the loose pronouns, you know what I mean. My job is to keep you functioning, and, if possible, free part of the time—holding the juggler's plates in the air, as the Hunter so aptly puts it—until all this is accomplished."

"It could be said more encouragingly, but that's right as far as you go," conceded Bob. "You do have one other job. Somehow PFI will have to be persuaded to use me in some way that won't either kill me too soon or reveal my medical problems to too many people. You can't just say I'm not able to work. Old Toke takes a big interest in people, and I can imagine his shipping me back to the States, or Japan, or wherever he happens to think I can get better medical attention than you can provide here. I mention this, of course, just to keep you from loafing between the shots of whatever you have to give me to keep me going."

"Phmph," snorted Seever. "Whatever I—"

"And in addition," the young man went on, "you'll really have to do something about Jenny."

"My daughter? Why? If you're falling in love with her I certainly don't object, but you'll have to do your own courting."

"Did you ever tell her about the Hunter and our adventures a few years ago? Or tell your wife so Jenny could have heard, or write any of it where she could have come across it to read?"

"No. None of those. I've wanted to tell Ev, but it isn't my secret. I will, if you and the Hunter ever let me. I've never written any of it anywhere."

"Then why did Jenny just now greet me, or us, with questions about lighting fuel oil fires? As I remember, she was away from Ell when we disposed of the Hunter's little problem—and she'd have been only about eleven then, anyway."

"That's right, she was." Seever was both puzzled and surprised. "I can't imagine what she's up to, or what she's found out, or how. If I talk in my sleep that coherently I'm sure Ev would have said something, and it still wouldn't explain Jenny's hearing me. Do you want to have her in and ask her right now, or have me ask her alone later on, or hold everything until you've done some thinking and investigating of your own?"

The Hunter expressed himself strongly in Bob's ear, but his host had reached the same conclusion independently and even more quickly.

"The last, by all means. I'd just as soon she didn't know we'd even mentioned it to you. We have no idea how much she knows, or why she's interested. If anyone starts asking her, she'll feel more certain she's onto something real—if she isn't certain already, of course. The only fire I can imagine her asking about is the one I lighted when we tricked the Hunter's quarry out of Dad's body—I can't remember ever lighting another that would mean anything special to anyone, at least. I can't see why she should be asking, if she never heard about it from anywhere."

"So," Seever cut in, "you're between Dilemma's right horn of needing to find out what she could have heard and where she could have heard it, and the left one of not wanting her to think that what she *has* heard means anything—if she doesn't already. I can see that, and will do my best not to make things any more confusing. I won't say anything to Jen if she doesn't start saying things to me. If she does, I'll find out what I can. You're right—she wasn't here that other time; she was in the hospital on Tahiti recovering from bone surgery I couldn't handle here, and her mother was with her. As you say, she was only eleven anyway. Someone else must have seen you light the fire, and must have told her, assuming there's any rational basis at all for her question. The alternative is not only unpleasant for me to consider, but calls for more coincidence than I can stomach." He paused in thought for several seconds. "Look," he said at length. "I promised not to say anything to her unless she spoke first, and I'll keep the promise unless you release me, but give this some thought. If I don't say anything to her, thereby implying that you didn't say anything to me about her fire questions, won't that itself be suspicious? Why *wouldn't* you have mentioned it to me? Shouldn't I question her, not as though she were poking into someone else's business, but as though I were wondering about *her* state of mind?"

The point seemed well taken, to the Hunter. Bob was less convinced.

"I can't stop you," he said slowly, "and don't want to hold you to a promise which goes against your judgment. So—well, do what you think is best. You certainly know her better than I do. The Hunter and I have to find those ships, and can't spend time yet finding out what Jenny's up to."

Seever raised an eyebrow; it seemed to him that his daughter's actions might be relevant enough to the current problem to deserve very close and immediate investigation. Bob failed to notice the change of expression, and the Hunter failed to see it clearly. His host's eyes were aimed in more or less the right direction, but the image of the doctor's face was not in their foveal region. The alien could make use of the less central parts of the retinas better than their owner could, but not perfectly; there was no remedy for the fact that the eye lenses did not focus perfectly.

"Somehow," Bob went on, "we've got to get hold of a boat. Dad's looking for diving gear and metal-finding equipment, but the ships certainly went down off the reef—at least, the Hunter's did, and that generator casing from the other turned up at a place which suggested it had been brought from outside. We'll need a reasonably good boat, because there'll be wind and surf problems out there."

Seever accepted the change of subject. "It'll need size, too, to carry air pumps and hoses and all that stuff," he said.

"Maybe not. Dad's going to try to find free-diving gear—the sort of stuff that fellow Cousteau has been developing. I was pricing it back in the States, but couldn't afford it or I'd have brought a set with me."

"Maybe the company has some."

"Dad was going to check that. Even if it does, though, I'll have trouble using their stuff full time."

"You'll have trouble doing anything full time except work for PFI. I may be able to clear you from heavy muscle work or fix you up so you can do it, but I don't see you spending eight hours a day poking around on the ocean bottom outside the reef. Thorvaldsen is very pro basic research, but your project would hardly fit anything he's likely to have in mind."

The Hunter and his host had talked this situation over at great length, and Bob was able to respond promptly.

"We've had some ideas on that. Remember, I have an even better certainty-that-it-can-be-done about both fusion power and faster-than-light travel than Toke had about biological engineering back in the twenties, when he started PFI. I'm as certain about them as the Russians were about the nuclear bomb— they didn't have to steal anything; when we used it, we'd given them free the only bit of knowledge whose lack might have kept them from making their own. If I could convince Old Toke that I really had something in either line, he'd probably back me carte blanche for basic research. There are only two troubles. One is that I'll have to solve my medical difficulties *first*, before I'll really have much to show him; and second, I can't honestly tell him either that I know how the Hunter's people do these things, or that they'll start giving up technical information hand over fist after they've cured me. In fact, as the Hunter admits, they'd probably be very cagey about letting me or any other human being learn many details for a generation or so, even after they open Earth up to symbiosis—if they do. I don't like the idea of deceiving the old guy for several reasons, not the least of which is my doubt that I'd get away with it.

"Of course, this just may be my uneasiness about

telling anyone about the Hunter and his people anyway; every time I think of it, I think of the word spreading that R. N. Kinnaird has lost his marbles."

"You know I could prove your story," Seever pointed out. "I did to your parents."

"You'd be taking a chance. Not everyone has been cured of synthetic pneumonia by a lump of green jelly, and not everyone who learned about the jelly would react in a nice, friendly, rational manner. I don't want to sound too paranoid, but I can see people who learned about the Hunter resenting my advantages, and—"

"Your present 'advantages' are hardly targets of jealousy."

"We're assuming my problems are going to be solved—remember? I'm trying to take the long view. Let's make the spreading of the word to the upper echelons the very last string to the bow, and concentrate on finding a decent boat."

"With no diving gear at all, even the self-contained sort you mentioned, what hurry is there for a boat? Surface diving off the reef won't let you search below three or four fathoms, and even that would take roughly forever," Seever pointed out.

"Of course. And I couldn't do much in one day without wearing myself out, unless you can do something about these weakness attacks. That wasn't the idea. Do you remember that piece of metal the fellows and I found out on one of the reef islands—the one that almost got Kenny Rice drowned?"

"I remember your telling me about it. You said it was a generator casing or something like that from one of the ships. I never saw it myself."

"That's it. We want to find it again, and let the Hunter check it over more carefully. He thinks he can get some idea of how far the other one traveled with it. He'll try to move it around himself under water to get some idea of the effort involved, maybe even backtrack. That thing certainly wouldn't have dragged very freely through the coral."

"Won't the coral have grown enough in the last seven or eight years to make that sort of detailed study pretty futile?"

"Maybe, but the Hunter thinks it's worth doing, and I agree. At least it will help us narrow down possibilities until we get the diving gear. Of course, any other ideas which anyone gets will be welcome, too."

Seever sighed. "All right," he agreed, "let's get down to my strictly medical part of the problem. Let me take a blood sample, not that I have all the lab equipment I'd like, and I'll see if I can get any ideas from what I don't find in you." His expression was clearly pessimistic. "There's one sort of known illness which vaguely resembles what you describe, and I've heard of a drug which might possibly help the symptoms. Just to make you happy, there's no claim it will touch the cause, which no one has yet identified. Of course, I don't have the drug here."

"Where would you have to send for it?" asked Bob. "The States?"

"Japan would probably be faster."

"Is it something you ever use? I mean, will anyone here get suspicious if you order it?"

"Don't get paranoid, youngster. No one ever checks on what I order. I'm my whole department. There's no one on Ell who would react to the name 'neostigmine' even if he saw the order, except maybe Old Toke himself. If you really want to worry, devote your thoughts to the fact that I'm only guessing it may help. Maybe I'll get more ideas from your blood, but don't count on it. Even though the Hunter is a detective, not a biochemist, and has grown up with a nonhuman species, he must know more about human physiology and biochemistry than I do. If he tells you to do anything, do it; don't wait for my advice."

The Hunter knew that Seever was right, but rather regretted his having brought up the point. Bob's morale was already quite low enough, and keeping him alive was already hard enough. Trying to keep the young chemist's hopes up was complicated by his intelligence; anything encouraging, to be worth saying, had to be reasonable. He and the Hunter had talked, long before and very briefly, of the possibility of finding the fugitive's ship and learning enough from it to let them build a larger one capable of taking Bob himself to Castor. Bob had dismissed the notion out of hand; it had been perfectly obvious to him that the job would have been analogous to a Cro-Magnon man's trying to copy an airplane engine. It was not a matter of native intelligence, but of the culture's background knowledge.

"I'll take blood from inside the right elbow, Hunter, if you want to get out of the way," Seever said as he approached with a large syringe. "I won't bother with the ligature if you'll supply a little back pressure on the vein." The Hunter agreed, Bob nodded, and seconds later the doctor had his sample.

"What now?" he asked. "Have you started to feel that fatigue yet today?"

"Nope, not yet. All I've done is bike down here, of course."

"What are you going to do now? Start looking for a boat, or entertain your sister?"

"She's in school for a few more hours, thank goodness. It's a pity vacation starts so soon. I'm just as bothered how to keep her little nose out of this project as I am about keeping it secret from the rest of the island—I suppose those amount to the same thing; if she knows, she'll tell her friends. However, we'll play that by ear. The first problem is a boat."

"What happened to the one your bunch used to have?"

"It sort of died of old age. The last time it started to fall apart, none of us had the time to fix it."

"Well, I have a suggestion, but you may not like it."

"What?"

"Jenny has a boat—more of a canoe, really—that she might be willing to lend."

"Without being told the whole story? I can't believe it."

"Oh, I wouldn't say she was that feminine," the father chuckled.

"I wasn't thinking about her sex, I'm assuming she's human. I wouldn't lend one of my own without a pretty good idea of what the borrower wanted it for. I was expecting to *buy* one so as to be able to use it without anyone's being entitled to ask what I was doing with it. Going outside the reef and working close in can be risky, especially with the wind from the west, and the owner would have every right to wonder if my head was on straight. Certainly Jenny would, if she's wondering about me already. You sure she hasn't been asking you about me?"

Seever's expression changed as he thought for a moment.

"Well, now that I think of it, she has; but there was nothing about fire in her questions. I mentioned a few weeks ago, at dinner I think, that my old-young friend Bob Kinnaird was going to be back from college before long, and she did put a question or two. I don't remember just how she worded them, now, but they seemed perfectly ordinary to me at the time. She never did know you very well, she'd been away at the time of the other problem, and I assumed she was wondering why I regarded you as a friend rather than just another patient."

Bob thought for several seconds, without consulting the Hunter.

"Maybe I *had* better talk to her about the boat. It will be an excuse for talking, and maybe this fire business will start to make some sense. All right if I call her in?"

Seever nodded agreement, but things didn't work out quite as expected. The moment Bob opened the door to the reception room, he and the Hunter saw several people waiting. Jenny promptly nodded to one of these, who as promptly rose and headed for the examining room, leaving Bob with nothing to do but hold the door for her.

The situation also left him with little to say, except

the basic request which was intended to start a longer inquiry. For a moment Bob wondered whether he should even do that; he asked the Hunter inaudibly, "Should we wait?" The alien advised him to ask about the boat anyway, since one was so badly needed. Bob almost nodded, but remembered in time.

"Jen," he asked, "your dad says you have a boat, and I need one for a while. Can I come back after office hours and see you about borrowing it?"

Jenny hesitated, too. Both Bob and the symbiont felt that the question, for some reason, surprised her.

"There aren't any real hours. Dad's open all the time, but I'm generally through by four or so. Come back then if you want. But tell me—have you been talking to that stringy towhead Malmstrom?"

"I met him when I landed yesterday just before sundown, and we talked old times for a few minutes until my folks showed up."

"He didn't say anything about my boat?"

"No. Why should he? Is it only for the use of blond males over six feet three inches, or something? I could bleach my hair a little, but I don't see how I can get five inches taller." Bob had taken a chance, the Hunter felt, asking questions which might lead to project-related answers with other people present, but Bob himself felt otherwise. He was sure that Jenny, whatever she said, would keep some sort of control in public; and the need for doing so might, he felt, distract her from the job of concealing things from *him*. It didn't work, however.

"No," was all she said. "Forget it. I'll talk to you later." The four people in the waiting room had obviously been listening, and at least two of them were openly amused. Jenny glared at one of these, a girl about her own age, went back to her desk, and very pointedly busied herself with her paper work. Bob tried to catch her eye, but she didn't look up, and after a few seconds he left.

Outside, he steered the bicycle toward the dock, rather than back home.

"You know," he muttered to his guest with less than impressive originality, "there's something queer going on. I wish I could guess whether it has anything to do with us or not. Her question about fire suggests it does, but that's all. I could believe she was having some sort of feud with Shorty—"

"Which needn't be connected with the fire matter at all," cut in the alien.

"True." Bob's train of thought was momentarily derailed, and he brooded silently as they rolled down the road. Finally he said more firmly, "Maybe we'd better hunt up Shorty and get another piece or two to this jigsaw." The Hunter agreed that this was sensible, but it did them no good; Malmstrom was not to be found.

It was Friday and he should have been working, but that did not help in locating him. Both working times and working places tended to be variable on Ell, since the population was small and the work had to be done when it had to be done. Malmstrom was still part of the youngest and least skilled section of the work force—what Bob thought of as a "hey-you" —and he might literally be anywhere on the island. However, some places were more likely than others.

He was not at the seaplane float, where the Catalina was moored unattended. Bob remembered that Dulac had said he was to have this day off. Malmstrom was not anywhere around the refinery and pumping station at the end of the dock. There was no tanker in that day, so the pumps were idle, but the refining section was always busy; it took the best part of an hour to make sure the one they sought wasn't there. This partly because of the changes which had taken place since Bob's boyhood; the refinery had expanded and grown much more complex during the Korean troubles. To the original marine fuels and lubricants which had once been the principal products of the organization, there had been added the more volatile liquids needed to slake the enormous thirst of jet engines; and more recently still, raw materials for plastics had been placed on the list.

The same expansion was noticeable along the northeast leg of the island, where they went next. There were more culture tanks; the distillation plant had been duplicated; and new and faster-growing vegetation covered the areas devoted to tank fodder. There were plenty of people at work, but Malmstrom was not among them.

He could, of course, have been at any of the tanks which dotted the lagoon. He could have been somewhere on the longer northwest leg of the island, though none of the industry was located here—it was all residential where it wasn't jungle. He might, Bob admitted to his companion, be hiding out from work anywhere around the lagoon, though that seemed unlikely. Everyone on the island was a PFI shareholder from birth, and the general attitude toward parasites was very negative.

The search ended just before noon, when Bob's muscles gave out. Neither he nor the Hunter was particularly surprised. There was nothing to be done about it but rest. They were near the northeast tip of the main island at this point, on a slope with the coral reef running out straight ahead of them, the lagoon to their left, and the empty Pacific to the right. There were no houses in this part of Ell, though parts of three culture tanks could be seen behind the ridge. They were on the road, which was narrow here and closely bordered by fodder-plants—the quick-growing stuff which was constantly being harvested and dumped into the culture tanks to feed the hydrocarbon-producing bacteria. There was no one in sight, which was a relief to both of them.

Lying down was distasteful but unavoidable; Bob had to rest. The soil consisted largely of tank sludge, and was one reason there were no residences at this end of the island. The smell was as offensive to the Hunter as to his host; the former avoided it by withdrawing from Bob's lungs—where he usually left a small part of his tissue directly exposed to the incoming oxygen—and making do with that available in the blood stream. The alien's need for the element was small except when he was operating independently of a host.

"It's an awful place to rest, and I know it bothers you too, but there's not much else we can do," Bob said as he settled down beside the bicycle. "I'll have to get back into at least walking condition if we're to keep that date with Jenny this afternoon."

"Perhaps we could make the doctor's house from here by going on foot very slowly," the symbiont suggested. "At least, shouldn't we try? He would certainly want to examine you in this condition, I'm sure, and even if you haven't recovered by four o'clock you could still talk to the young woman."

"Two miles? Forget it. Besides, if I walked in like this—or more probably crawled in—she'd have to have some explanation."

"I've been thinking about that," the symbiont replied. "If you use her boat, you'll probably have to explain a lot anyway, as you yourself were saying to her father. Also, you can't go alone to do the searching; neither your parents nor the doctor will be available for help much of the time; it's her boat, she'll probably want to go along with us at least part of the time, and we're going to have trouble finding a convincing reason why she shouldn't. Bob, I know you like it much less than I do—after all, I'm merely following a reasonable regulation which can legally be violated if circumstances demand it, while you are quite reasonably afraid of being thought crazy or a liar by people who don't get the story first-hand and with all the evidence; but I am getting resigned to the idea that we are going to need several more of your people in this operation with us—fully informed."

"You can really get away with breaking your regulations?"

"I would have to justify my actions, but we tend to have much respect for the judgment of the man in the field. I have already exercised that discretion with you, the doctor, and your parents, and am not worried about any penalties when we are rescued. I am quite certain that none of you will let out the word in such broadcast fashion as to interfere with the work of any exploring team. I do believe, now, that a few more members of this in-group are going to be needed to save your life—which I regard as much more important than holding certain principles inviolate."

"And you think Jenny is a good prospect?" asked Bob.

"I don't know. She should be useful; she is clearly intelligent or she could not be doing the work she does for her father. She appears physically strong— she is nearly as tall as you, and I judge not much lighter. If she uses this boat of hers very much, I feel safe in assuming that a reasonable fraction of the weight is muscle. Another point from the work she does—her father evidently trusts her discretion, or she wouldn't be doing his medical records. Your species has what I consider an exaggerated idea of the importance of privacy in such matters. Think it over— but I think I'm right."

Bob did not think for very long; he fell asleep. This was one of the most inconvenient human habits, from the Hunter's viewpoint. He himself could not sleep in anything like the human fashion; he remained conscious as long as the oxygen supply was adequate. His humanoid hosts on his home world spent less than a tenth of their time in sleep, and the cultural situation was based on this fact and provided activities for the small symbionts during these periods.

When, and if, Bob's medical problem was solved, the Hunter knew that he would have to work out some rather difficult details about their partnership. Presumably the examination team, if it decided to join up with humanity, would have solutions to offer.

At the moment, he could do something. The surrounding vegetation was strange to him—the breeds were always being replaced with new ones by the biological engineers—and there existed a small chance that something useful in the medical problem might be present. The Hunter extended a fairly large pseudopod through the skin of his host's hand and gathered in some of the material, pulling it close against the skin, digesting it, and checking the breakdown products for new materials. A few seemed promising, and samples of their molecules were absorbed through Bob's pores and between the cells of the inner skin layers for local, very careful testing of their biological effects. The Hunter himself did not leave his own tissue outside for long; sunlight drove him back inside. The Castor C twin suns produced strong ultraviolet only during the aperiodic flare times, and he could stand very little of it.

He devoted the rest of the sleep to investigation. He had to experiment; dangerous as it might be, ignorance was even more so. He increased and decreased hormone secretion, trying to decide when one or another was not only doing a primary job but also affecting the flow of still others . . .

It *was* detective work, but he wished he had studied biochemistry more carefully a couple of human lifetimes ago.

4. Arrangements and People

Robert Kinnaird woke up with the weakness gone for the moment, but with a brand new trouble to consider. He had not eaten since breakfast, their search not having taken them anywhere near his home, and he had a completely empty stomach, for which the Hunter could vouch. For some reason, however, he was feeling an extreme nausea. The suggestion, even the thought, of eating made him double up, almost out of control. He didn't dare ride in that condition, having no confidence in his ability not to think of food, so they set off toward the village on foot, wheeling the machine.

After a mile or so the sensation wore off, but since they did not know the cause and couldn't be sure it would not come back, they decided against riding.

The road was wider, with buildings now quite frequent on either side; the Hunter saw and remembered the one which had figured in the flaming climax of their adventure seven years before. As they approached this structure, a child of about ten or eleven appeared from behind it, watched them silently until they were in front of him, and then fell in beside them. The Hunter was curious, but could not take a good look while Bob was keeping his eyes on the ground.

The group walked another hundred yards or so before the youngster spoke. Then he asked abruptly, "What's wrong with the bike?"

"Nothing," answered Bob, looking directly at him for the first time.

"Why aren't you riding it?"

"Why do you care?" The child looked startled at first, then rather resigned.

"No special reason." He didn't quite shrug his shoulders, but somehow gave the impression that he felt like it. "Just curious. If you don't want to tell me, don't."

Bob pulled himself out of his negative mood and said, "Sorry. I've been having stomach cramps, so I couldn't ride and felt terrible, but I shouldn't take it out on you."

"That's all right. Going to the doctor's?"

"Yes, it seems a good idea. Wouldn't you?"

The conversation dropped. The Hunter had had his good look at the youngster, but hadn't gained much by it. The only even slightly unusual characteristic of the child was his weight. The Ell children tended to run lean, since a high level of physical activity was the accepted thing. This one was not really plump, but by island standards was decidedly heavy for his height. His features and complexion were standard for the island, a mixture of Polynesian and European; his skin was brown, hair black, eyes blue, nose and chin rather sharp. He wore the usual shorts which were equally stylish in or out of the water.

There was simply nothing remarkable about him, and neither Bob nor the Hunter gave him another thought, for a few minutes. Their attention was completely diverted from him when another bicycle pulled up beside them to reveal that their morning's search was over. Kenneth Malmstrom was with them.

"Hi, Bob. Just heading home for lunch? Mine was late, too."

"I'd sort of forgotten about eating," Bob responded. "Been riding all over the place to make myself at home again. I'd like to do the same on the water, maybe tomorrow. Too bad the others aren't with us—and the old boat."

"I'd go, but I'm not free this weekend—at least, I'm not exactly working, but I have to stay in hearing of a phone tomorrow. I suppose you'll want to go anyway, before you start work too. Any idea when that'll be?"

"Well, Doc checked me over this morning. Unless he finds something out of line, I suppose Monday. I wouldn't know where or what. If you're not free tomorrow or Sunday, I might as well row a bit by myself, if I can find a boat.

"Lots of those around," Malmstrom assured him. "I'd let you have mine, but I sold it to a kid over a year ago—didn't have enough time for it to make it worth the upkeep work. Speaking of boats and fun— *you*, André. Have you been around the airplane again?"

"When?" The boy who had been standing silently beside them seemed neither surprised nor indignant at the question.

"Any time since it got here yesterday, but especially this morning. You remember what you got told after you tied the wheel struts to the float under water, where no one could see the rope?"

"I remember." Bob, with the memory of his father's injury the night before rising in his mind, looked at the child with interest; but neither he nor the Hunter could read anything from André's expression. There was certainly no fear, and no really obvious amusement. Malmstrom was not trying to analyze; he already had his suspicions, and intended to air them.

"Well, someone's done it again. I hope no one's seen you around with a length of rope, or you're in trouble."

"They haven't. I'm not." The young face remained expressionless. Malmstrom eyed the boy sternly for half a minute, but got nothing for his trouble and finally returned to the earlier subject.

"I sometimes miss the old boat, but there are plenty around—you can always borrow one."

"So I gather," replied Bob. "The Doc said his girl had one she might be willing to lend; I'll go back after I eat and—what's so funny?" Malmstrom was grinning broadly.

"Doc's a swell guy," he chuckled, "but he's too fond of Jenny. She can't do anything wrong—ask him. Wait till you see the boat. She made it herself."

"So? Don't most people? What's wrong with it?"

"She used some kind of kit she sent away for. It's mostly canvas. I wouldn't get into it for money."

"Did you tell her that? Did she ask you to ride in it?"

"No, she sure didn't. I've been kidding her ever since she started making it."

"I see. Well, I'll be seeing Doc again anyway, but thanks for the warning. I'll use my judgment about Jenny's boat. See you later; I'm hungry."

"And I'm late. So long." The tall youth pedaled rapidly away in the direction from which the others had come, and all three looked after him thoughtfully.

"He's pretty dumb," the child suddenly volunteered.

"Why?" asked Bob. "He found out about your tying up the airplane, the other time."

"No, he didn't. He couldn't find his own nose if it was after dark. Someone told him I did that, and now he blames everything on me."

"And he's never right?"

"Sometimes. A busted clock is right twice a day." There was still no expression behind the words or on the face.

"Is he right about Jenny Seever's boat?"

"You said you'd see for yourself." There might have been reproach in the child's tones, this time. Bob was somewhat amused, and the Hunter was developing a real interest in André. He, too, had thought about the incident of the footlocker.

Bob had resumed wheeling the bicycle toward the doctor's. André accompanied them as far as the road which led down to the dock. He turned down this way while the others went on, eventually reaching the Kinnaird home.

Bob's mother had expected them much earlier and had obviously been worried; her son made excuses and apologies without mentioning the fatigue attack. As he ate, he gave a somewhat edited report of his talk with Seever, mentioned that he and the Hunter had bicycled around much of the island, and eventually spoke of the possibility of using Jenny's canoe.

"Do you know anything about that, Mom?" he asked. "We met Shorty Malmstrom just before we got here, and when I said something about Jenny's boat he nearly split. He said he'd never want to ride in it. She didn't strike me as exactly incompetent; is she?"

"I don't believe so," his mother answered. "I know the Seevers very well, of course; Ben and Ev are probably our best friends. Jenny took care of Daphne quite often when she was very small. I never heard anything about her boat, or about any fuss between her and Shorty. Of course, there could be some story current among the teen-age set that I might never have heard; you should check with someone younger. Even Daphne might know more than I."

No opportunity of consulting his sister arose, however; she seemed to have gone with friends after school, and her mother did not expect her until suppertime. Bob rested until nearly four, and then headed back to the Seevers'. He used the bicycle, but not without some hesitation and discussion with the Hunter. It might delay the onset of the next fatigue attack; on the other hand, it would be a nuisance if the nausea struck again. The Hunter could not even guess which was more likely to happen, since he had not yet come up with a specific cause for either, so he voted for speed.

There were still patients in the waiting room when they arrived, and Jenny was still at her desk. When she saw Bob, however, she slipped the papers in front of her into a folder, rose, and came toward him.

"Let's go," she said. "I'll show you the boat, if you still want it."

"What about the other people here?" asked Bob in some surprise.

"They don't need me. It's Dad they're after. Did you think he'd gotten so formal that everyone has to be escorted from waiting room to office?"

"It looked like it this morning."

"Not the story. He expects me to be useful and tactful—"

"And decorative?" Her eyes, little more than two inches below his, swept over his face for a moment, but she showed no other sign of being impressed by the remark.

"That wasn't mentioned, thanks. As long as the records are straight and he can find anything he wants, I'm earning my dividend."

They were outside now, and Bob gestured toward the bicycle rack. "Walk or wheel?"

"Walk. Most of the way is on sand." She led the way, not toward the road leading down to the dock, but almost directly toward the water, threading among houses and gardens along the narrow paths which separated them. The girl seemed to feel no need of conversation, and the Hunter was perfectly willing to think rather than listen. Bob, however, felt that time was not a commodity he could afford to waste.

"We saw Shorty just before lunch. What does he have against you, anyway?"

The girl stopped and faced him, somehow looking even taller. "Do you want the boat?" she asked curtly.

"I won't know until I've seen it, and probably not until I've tried it," Bob retorted. His tone showed annoyance; the Hunter knew he was acting, but Jenny fortunately did not. "D'you think I let Shorty do my thinking for me? I asked what he had against *you,* not your canoe."

"I suppose you wouldn't." Jenny appeared to relax, and resumed the way toward the shore. "I don't know why he's like that. I got the plans for the boat by mail, and the first time he saw me working on it he offered to help—actually he said he 'could do it for me.' I said I'd rather see whether I could do it for myself, and I haven't heard a polite word from him in a year and a half. He keeps asking me if it's had moths, or a run in the bottom, or a lot of other things he seems to think are funny. I won't blame you for your friends, but don't expect me to have much use for that one."

"Maybe he felt insulted by your refusing his help."

"Maybe so. I certainly felt insulted by the way he offered it—as though I didn't have a chance of doing it right by myself. I don't know whether he felt that way because I'm female, or just because my name isn't Kenneth Malmstrom and I'm less than six and a quarter feet high."

"Knowing Shorty, I'd guess the latter," Bob soothed. "He was sometimes that way with the rest of us, but we didn't take him very seriously. If he got too bumptious it was usually easy enough to come up with a put-down hard enough to hold him for three or four weeks. I thought he'd pretty well outgrown that, though, the last time I was home."

"Maybe he has, with you. Putting him down doesn't work for me. He knows I did a good job with the kayak, he's seen it, he's seen lots of people use it, but whenever he sees it or me he makes remarks. I bet he did when you saw him today."

"Very vague ones. As I said, I'll make up my mind when I see the boat. If you and other people have been using it for a year and a half I won't worry about the thing itself, but I still have to judge whether it's big enough for what I need."

"What's that? Or don't you think I'd understand?"

"Why shouldn't you? I have to look for some special things. One of them is, or used to be, out on one of the reef islands, Apu. Anything that'll carry me there will do. The other is under water, almost certainly outside the reef, and I'll need a boat that I can dive from when my equipment gets here."

"You mean pumps and that sort of thing? My kayak can't carry anything like that."

"No, I mean free diving, with personal mask and air tank. You may have read about it."

"I have. You're getting that?"

"When I can afford it, unless Dad can come through earlier. I'm short on paydays so far."

"That should be fun. I've thought of doing it ever since I heard about it. Can I go with you?" Bob had expected the question, of course, but had failed to plan a very farsighted answer.

"You mean alternate dives with me, or something like that? I can afford only one outfit."

Jenny stopped and looked at him again, this time with her lips pursed into a schoolma'amish expression.

"I realize that Shorty Malmstrom must have been named from his brains, not his height, but I bet even he wouldn't think of going free-diving alone. Do you have more lives than money, or what? Maybe I shouldn't trust you with my boat, after all."

Even the Hunter was startled. Bob was dumbfounded. Incredibly, neither of them had thought of this particular safety question, in spite of the Hunter's awareness of the human tendency to crowd the experience limit, and also in spite of his fear of what that tendency might do to his host—and his knowledge of what it had done, luckily for the Hunter himself, to his host's father.

The simple insanity of Bob's working under water with only the Hunter with him had never crossed either of their minds; the fact was that there was nothing the Hunter could do about drowning. He could make a fairly effective gill system out of his own tissue, but there was only four pounds of that and a human being needs a lot of oxygen. It was possible that the Hunter could keep his host alive for a time under water, but probably not conscious and certainly not active, especially in warm water. The solubility of gases, including oxygen, goes down with rising temperature.

"You're right!" Bob gasped. "We'd forgotten all about that—at least," he tried to recover what he thought was a slip, and hesitated a moment before he saw the way—"at least *I* forgot; maybe Dad thought of it and didn't say anything. We *will* have to get two sets—and it'll have to be only two, at first. We can't put off the search until I can afford more."

"Then it's important," Jenny said.

"Yeah. Life and death, to be trite." The Hunter was almost certain that his host was by now convinced of the need for more help, though nothing more had been said on the subject since the discussion at midday. The alien had convinced himself that Jenny would be a good recruit. He had not intended to exert any more pressure on his human companion, but couldn't resist at this point.

"You're going to have to tell her," he vibrated into Bob's ears.

"She'll think I'm crazy as Shorty. We'll hold off just a little." The vocal cords just barely oscillated, but the alien was ready for the message. He couldn't shrug Bob's shoulders, but was tempted to try.

Aloud, Bob said to Jenny, "I think I can tell you

more a little later. It's not entirely my own secret."
This was technically true, but once again misleading
enough to bother the Hunter slightly. "I'll tell you a
little—my own part of it. There's a problem which will
kill me if it isn't solved fairly soon. Your father knows
about it, since it's partly medical, but I don't want to
tell you details until I've talked to him and one other
person. I hope you don't mind."

"I do, a little, but I won't fight it. Do your own
folks know?"

"My parents do. Not Silly."

"All right. I'm curious enough to light matches between your toes, but I guess I can wait. I warn you
I'll pry anything I can out of Dad. Of course he
doesn't talk about patients' affairs, but there are
ways."

"Do your best." Bob was actually pleased with the
answer. He would be delighted if she could actually
get the story from some source other than himself;
that way, whether she believed it or not, there would
at least be no doubts about his own sanity. The
Hunter hadn't thought of that side of the question,
but was pleased at the general trend of affairs.

Bob wondered briefly whether he should try to get
word to the doctor before his daughter reached him,
but decided there was nothing to be gained. Medical
ethics would of course tend to keep Seever quiet; if
his daughter was smart enough to get through that
barrier, she would presumably be smart enough to be
helpful to him and the Hunter.

The boat looked all right. It was different enough
from most of those on the island to show the Hunter
and his host why Malmstrom, not in the habit of deep
or thoughtful analysis of the things he saw, might consider it funny. Small and double-ended, it consisted
essentially of a canvas-covered wooden frame. Consequently, it was very light.

"It's called a kayak, in case you've never seen anything like it." Jenny spoke rather nervously as they
looked it over; she was clearly afraid that Bob would

react as Malmstrom had. "I made it from a kit I got by mail from the States. It's good and steady, and I've had it outside the reef plenty of times with no trouble."

"It looks fine to me," Bob assured her. "One thing —it's light, and must ride pretty high when it's empty or has only one passenger. Could a diver climb back aboard without capsizing it?"

"Sure. I swim from it a lot, and have no trouble getting back in. It's a trick, but I'll show you."

"Okay. Then if you'll let me use it, I'll look over Apu tomorrow. I'd do it right now if we had more than an hour or so to sunset."

"May I come with you? Or don't you want me to see what you're looking for?"

"Even money she'll know by then, anyway," the Hunter muttered to his host. The latter hesitated, looking thoughtfully at the young woman. She looked back at him steadily; the nervous, defensive attitude had disappeared.

"Is that a condition for using the boat?" Bob asked at length. She shook her head negatively, confirming the Hunter's opinion of her intelligence. As Bob fell silent again for several seconds, she removed the broad-brimmed hat which shielded her rather pale skin from the sun, and let her mahogany-red hair blow free. To do her justice, she was not consciously using the good looks of which she was fully aware in an effort to influence the young man's decision. This was just as well, since neither Bob nor the Hunter was giving the slightest thought to that aspect of the matter. Her five feet eight inches of height and one-hundred-and-twenty-plus pounds of weight had probably never produced less effect on a male observer.

"All right," Bob said at last. "The sun will be up by a quarter to seven. Can you be here by then?"

"Sure. Do you want to try out the boat, now?"

"Why not? That double paddle looks as though it might take practice."

"Can I come too?" came another voice. Bob turned abruptly, and saw the small boy who had accosted him earlier in the day. Jenny showed no surprise, having seen him approach. She answered the question without consulting Bob by voice or glance.

"All right, André. Ride forward when we get it in the water."

"Can I paddle?"

"Some of the time. Bob needs practice, first."

Dropping her hat on the sand, Jenny lifted the kayak onto her head, refusing with a gesture Bob's offer of help. The child made no such offer, not even bothering to pick up the hat.

Bob kicked off his sneakers and rolled up his trouser legs, retrieved the hat, and handed it to Jenny as she set the kayak down in calf-deep water. She had not bothered to keep slacks or sandals dry; she simply seated herself in the middle of the small craft, nodded Bob to the stern, waited until André had splashed past them and settled himself in the bow, and then started to paddle.

Without looking back, she remarked, "You'd better wear something more tomorrow. You probably tan better than I do, but with no hat and that T-shirt your arms and face will be in pretty bad shape before the day's over. You've been out of the sun for a long time."

"Good point," Bob admitted. There was silence for several minutes while the girl maneuvered the little craft forward and backward, and turned it both ways at varying speeds. Finally she handed the paddle back to Bob.

"It'll be easier from there," she assured him. He found no great difficulty in mastering the little canoe, as his extensive experience with rowboats was not wholly irrelevant—Newton's third law is very, very general. The girl gave an occasional word of advice, but on the whole he had no trouble making the little vessel behave.

"I don't see what Shorty has against this," he said at length. The boy in front spoke without turning his head.

"I told you. He's stupid." Bob managed to contain his amusement.

"You and Jenny must be good friends," Bob suggested.

"I've known André most of his life," the girl said. "I used to baby-sit for him and his sisters. We're good friends most of the time."

"He likes your boat, anyway."

"Don't you?"

"Sure. It's fine. It should do for the diving, too, if we have only two people in it."

"If two go down, we'll need a third to handle the boat," Jenny pointed out. Bob grew thoughtful, and was silent for a few seconds.

"Well, we'll try," he said at length. "Anyway, the gear will be a long time coming, I'm afraid."

"You're going to go diving? With suits?" André asked excitedly. "I can handle the kayak. Let me be with you!"

"Maybe," Jenny said. "It's Bob's business. You'll have to convince him he wants you. I can tell him how good you are with the kayak, but you'll have to be careful not to spoil anything." Both Bob and the Hunter could tell that some meaning lay under the rather elaborate remark. Both tended to connect it with Malmstrom's charges of malicious mischief earlier in the day. It was some time before they learned how wrong, and at the same time how right, they were.

"Let André paddle now, if he wants," Bob said suddenly. He handed the implement forward to Jenny, who passed it on. "The sun's nearly down. Bring us ashore where we were, unless Jenny wants the boat somewhere else."

The child obeyed silently. The Hunter knew why Bob had given up the paddle; the fatigue had struck again. He was having trouble holding on to the tool, to say nothing of driving the vessel with it. They were half a mile from the beach; the alien hoped, somewhat forlornly, that his companion would get enough rest in the few minutes it would take to get ashore to permit normal operation as far as the doctor's home.

André left as soon as they reached the shore, without helping get the canoe out of the water. Jenny did this unassisted; Bob had two reasons for not offering his muscles—she had, after all, refused help before. The walk to the Seevers' was made slowly and in silence; Bob had recovered a little, and hoped the girl wasn't noticing his weakness. At any rate, she made no comment on it.

It was getting dark now, and he needed no excuse to walk the bicycle home instead of riding it up the northwest road.

The early part of the evening, while Daphne was still up, passed without particular incident. The child noticed her brother's fatigue, but he managed to pass it off by saying that he was out of condition and had tried to get around too much of the island. Even the Hunter had no moral objection to this. Daphne was not very sympathetic, and both Bob and the Hunter foresaw some trouble if the drug Seever had mentioned failed to come soon and do some good.

When the child disappeared for the night, Bob made a fairly complete report of the day's doings, not stressing the fatigue attacks. His decision, now crystallized, to bring Jenny onto the working team was approved by both parents—they did not feel strongly either way about the girl herself, but were in favor of anything that promised to speed up the project.

Mrs. Kinnaird asked whether her friend Evelyn Seever might not also be included, and Bob admitted that the doctor had made hints in the same direction. It would be nice, he granted, if the two families were completely involved and free to discuss the problems without the need for finding an excuse to exclude some of the members.

"It's too bad Silly isn't older," he even admitted. "But at least, there's a good excuse for easing her out of the way at night."

"Then you'll let Ben tell Ev?" his mother persisted.

"Well—I guess so." Bob's attitude, almost reflexive

after more than seven years, was yielding; but it was putting up a good fight.

"I've sent for a couple of those free-diving outfits," said Bob's father, changing the subject. "We're going to have to improvise something to keep the tanks charged, I expect. We have a compressor for the pneumatic hammers and drills, but its connections and controls will have to be played with a bit."

"You ordered two?" Bob asked as indifferently as he could.

"Of course. You weren't planning to dive alone, I trust." Strictly out of kindness, the Hunter worked on Bob's facial capillaries to forestall the blush which was obviously coming. The younger man changed the subject, he hoped unobtrusively.

"I wonder how long they'll take to get here?"

"Don't hold your breath waiting. Even by air it's a long journey. There's nothing more we can do about it for now. You said something about getting hold of an old mine detector or something of that sort, didn't you?"

"Yes. It could save a lot of time, if the things will work under water."

"I don't think we'd have to send for that," said Arthur Kinnaird happily. "Taro Tavaké at the radio station can probably make one, considering his war background in the Solomons. I'm positive he knows how they work, from things he's said. I'll talk to him tomorrow."

Bob was appropriately gratified. "Good," he said brightly. "That seems to set us up for now. When the diving gear comes we'll have to make more detailed plans, but that will be a while."

"One thing," his mother put in. "Once you start work, when do you get all these things done? And who, besides your father, dives with you? You'll both have working hours which won't leave very much time free for this. Have you given any thought to taking Old Toke into the secret and having him assign you the job of finding spaceships? That would simplify a lot of things."

"We've thought of it and talked about it a lot, Mom. For now we've decided against it—only partly because I'm so much against telling anyone. Toke Thorvaldsen and his son both have a lot of influence, since they *are* PFI, and the Hunter's regulations apply a good deal more stiffly to people like them than they do to us."

"Even though it would improve our chances of saving your life?" the woman insisted.

"Believe me, we've thought it over, Mom. There are risks each way, and I've settled which ones I prefer. The Hunter agrees with me. I may be wrong, but that's the way I want to play it."

"And, as you kindly refrain from pointing out, it is your own game. Very well, Son, we'll try to play it on your side. You'll forgive us for worrying."

5. When in Doubt, Ask

Jenny reached the boat at almost the same moment as Bob and the Hunter. She nodded approvingly at his costume, almost exactly like her own—slacks, long-sleeved shirt, coolie hat, and old sneakers as protection against the coral. Unlike the man, she was carrying a mesh bag containing fruit.

"I don't expect much trouble finding what I want," Bob said as he noticed the food. "I wasn't counting on having to stay all day."

"I hope you're right," she answered, "but I'll still be happier if we have it with us. Now, are you going to tell me what we're looking for, or am I just the taxi driver?" She was letting Bob carry the kayak this time, and he was silent until it was in the water and they had climbed in. His first words were not an answer to her question.

"What did you find out from your father?"

"Nothing. I didn't ask him anything, and there's nothing in your medical record that helps."

"You looked at it, then."

"I told you I would."

"All right, here's the deal. I'll tell you the whole story, taking my chances that you'll decide I'm a fruitcake—only remember your dad can back it all up—if you'll fill me in on this fire-lighting business you started off with yesterday morning. I have to admit I'm wondering about that. All right?"

"Then the question did mean something to you."

"It certainly did. It fits into what I have to tell you, if that helps."

Jenny paddled silently for several strokes, and when she spoke it was not a direct answer.

"I wouldn't have said that was a fair deal for you, if you hadn't made that last remark," she said at last. "I never thought the fire question was very important, though I've been wondering about the answer for years. Maybe there's more to it than I thought, though, if it ties into a life-and-death matter for you. Anyway, here's the story from my side.

"I suppose you know the desChenes family—at least, you met André yesterday. Their father used to be on a tanker crew, but they gave him a shore job when his wife died seven years ago having a baby. There are two older children—André is the first—and a lot of us have taken care of them at one time or another. I'm afraid we haven't done the best job in the world, because André, to put it simply, is a pure pest. He really likes to bother and even hurt people. I know most kids go through that stage, but you expect them to be long past it by the time they're eleven. I think he's over the edge myself, but Dad says he's just had some unfortunately timed shocks and should get over it.

"Anyway, he thinks practical jokes are funny—really practical ones, like hot pennies down the neck and trip-strings on stairs, not just water buckets over the door. I've had one badly sprained ankle, at least half a dozen falls that didn't do so much damage, and I've put out three fires in the yard around his house—never inside, to give him credit. About four years ago—I was only fourteen, and it was the first time I'd had the kids all by myself while Mr. desChenes was at work—was the first of the fires, and of course I tried to explain to him why that wasn't such a good idea. He told me very solemnly that he really knew better. He didn't stop, though.

"The third time it happened, maybe a year and a half later, he got burned himself—not seriously, but enough to show him what it felt like. I thought the talking-to would really mean something that time. He was very indignant, not with me but with the fire. He insisted it wasn't fair that one person could play tricks with fire and have fun, while someone else who did it got hurt. It took me a couple of weeks, off and on, to find out what he was talking about. At last he told me about seeing a big boy pour a lot of oil on the ground and set fire to it, and seeing a car drive into the fire, and the boy jump into the car and drive it out again. Later still, a couple of years ago while you were home, I was with him and we happened to see you. He said you were the big boy who made the fire. I've never been sure what to believe, since his jokes sometimes include pretty fancy lies, and I've been wanting to find out ever since.

"There's one complication. As nearly as I could find out, this all happened the day his younger sister was born and his mother died. Maybe that's why it made such an impression on him, maybe not. Maybe nothing of the sort happened at all, but I'd like to know. I'm not especially fond of the kid, but it would be nice to unkink him."

"It happened about that way," Bob said thoughtfully. "Let's see—he was about four years old then. I didn't actually drive into the fire, but he might have had a bad view, or might just not remember." He fell silent; both he and the Hunter were badly jolted. Neither had had the slightest suspicion that there had been a witness to the settling of the earlier problem, other than Bob's father. Both were wondering how much of the story, and in what distorted forms, had been spread among the younger fraction of Ell's population.

"Too bad you didn't tell that to your father," Bob said at last. "I don't know what sort of psychologist he is, but at least you might have known the facts behind the story."

"Dad knows about it? He never—"

"He wouldn't. How could he? Yes, he knows."

"There's nothing about it in the folder he keeps on you."

"I know, Miss Secretary. I'll have to read that some time and find out what you *do* know about me. The fire-lighting was not a medical activity, and he has reasons for not writing down even all of my medical problems."

"Which you are about to tell me, I take it."

"If you like. If you think you can believe him more easily than you can me, go to your father and tell him I said he can tell you all about the Hunter. Which do you want?"

"Start talking. I'll check your version against Dad's when I see him."

The account took the rest of the journey to the small islet to satisfy the girl's need for detail, though the basic story went quickly enough. Her questions convinced the Hunter of what he had strongly suspected earlier—Jenny was quicker-minded than his own host. Naturally, she had trouble believing at first, and the alien rather expected her to demand the sort of proof her father had wanted years before. Instead, she made do with some very penetrating and well-thought-out questions. Some of these, about the alien's physical nature, Bob himself had never asked in the nearly eight years of their association. Most of them reflected the medical work she had been doing for her father, incidentally showing that she had been reading much more than his case records. This surprised Bob, who was freshly enough out of college to be inclined to look down on those who had not enjoyed the advantages of higher education.

"I didn't think she had all that," he muttered to his symbiont at one point. "There was never any talk that I heard about her using the college offer, or even going away from Ell for school." He was tactful enough not to let his surprise get into his words, but the Hunter could often detect it from his host's more subtle internal reactions. It pleased the alien; his friend, he felt, was getting more education, which was clearly needed.

The kayak was carried ashore and set well away from the water, though they were on the lee side of Apu and there were no waves to speak of from the lagoon side. Apu was one of the largest of the islets scattered along the Ell reef, and had collected enough soil over the years to support not only underbrush but several palms. Very little of the peculiar vegetation from the engineering laboratories, which covered so much of the long northwest arm of the main island, had escaped this far.

There was a beach on the lagoon side, but the outer face merged directly into the irregular, murderous coral of the reef itself, dangerous for a swimmer on the quietest days and suicidal with the slightest swell. The reef, defined as the region where coral grew close enough to the surface to influence wave patterns, extended hundreds of yards out to sea. It broke much of the violence of incoming waves, but complicated their pattern so as to make it impossible to tell when a particular spot along Apu's outer face would be under water the next moment. The Hunter and Bob both remembered vividly the time years before when Ken

Rice had gone down into one of the coral-rimmed bays to pick something up, and nearly been drowned. The "something" had not been recovered, but the Hunter had seen it clearly enough to identify a generator shield which must have come from his quarry's ship, and which had provided the first certainty that the other alien had come ashore at all.

It was this object they were seeking, in the hope that it would provide information which would narrow the search area for the missing ship of the fugitive. It was this vessel which promised more to the plan; the Hunter knew that his own vessel had been crushed almost flat, and might have been too completely corroded for detection even by the time the searchers might have come. The shield, on the other hand, had appeared intact, giving some promise that the ship it had come from had escaped such complete destruction.

The search was not easy. Coral grows, and waves destroy; the outer side of Apu had changed much. Bob and the Hunter remembered roughly where the near-drowning had occurred, but it took them more than fifteen minutes to narrow down to four the possibilities among the endless bays and coves. Even then they were far from sure; very close examination would be necessary.

They approached the first of these with caution; it was hurling spray far above their heads at irregular intervals as waves focused into it. Neither Bob nor the Hunter could identify its interior details with any certainty in the moments they could look. They had hoped that the gleam of metal might be visible, but that was not really reasonable after all these years. If this were the same notch, conditions had changed. Then, the boys had gone into it without hesitation; now, not even the most foolhardy of teen-agers would have taken the chance. They stayed with it as long as they did only because Jenny, who had only verbal description to go by, kept pointing at different features and asking whether this, or that, or the other thing might possibly be what they wanted. Unfortunately, while all were possibilities, none was encouraging enough to merit close investigation in that welter of foam and sharp coral.

The second of the possible spots was much quieter and less dangerous, but they spent even more time there. Several of the coral masses might, as far as appearance was concerned, be concealing the object of their search. Bob and Jenny had swimming suits under their outer clothes, and both went into the water to check these possibilities more closely. Bob of course could see much better under water than the girl, since the alien could extrude tissue to reshape his cornea for focusing in the different medium, but even with this help no sign of metal was detected.

At the third bay, Bob's fatigue caught up with him again, and Jenny had to help him out of the water. On the theory that food would provide energy, she insisted on his eating one of the fruits she had brought, and this triggered the nausea of the day before.

Jenny had not really accepted the fact that the situation was really a life-and-death one as far as Bob was concerned. She felt slightly superior about his need for her help in the water, and was even somewhat amused at the spectacle he made trying to eat. Neither Bob nor his symbiont fully understood her.

Serious or not, however, she insisted on finishing the check-out of the third cove by herself and, judging by the time she spent under water, must have done a fairly thorough job. She tried to make up for deficient underwater eyesight by using her sense of touch, and emerged finally with several cuts on hands and forearms, inflicted by the coral.

Then she wanted to do the fourth site alone, though it was much like the first in wave action.

"Don't be crazy!" Bob snapped when she made this proposal. "It's as dangerous as the one we passed up, and I'm not in shape to help you when you get in trouble. If we really knew the thing was there it might be different, but we're not sure enough for that sort of risk. Look from up here if you want, and tell us if you think anything looks hopeful, and then we'll decide what to do; but I think we're going to need that metal detector Dad is lining up even for this part of the search. If you go in there, you'll have to stop calling Shorty a nut."

"I suppose that's true," Jenny agreed reluctantly, "but I thought you considered this project important."

"I do. It's important enough not to lose any of the help. Get your clothes on; we don't want to lose anyone to sunburn, either." The redhead, in spite of her lifelong residence in the tropics, had skin even paler than Bob's, though she was heavily freckled.

"Maybe the Hunter ought to stay with me for a while, and protect the useful member of the team," she suggested.

"He can't do anything about sunburn—he can't stand ultraviolet even as well as we can," replied Bob.

"I was thinking about my hands," she retorted, looking at the oozing scratches.

"Well, the Hunter might leave me while I'm awake now that I know him so well, but he'd certainly wait until you were asleep before he went to you. He has definite ideas about how people who aren't used to symbiosis are likely to react to a puddle of green jelly flowing toward them; and if they pull him apart trying to get away while he's partly inside, he finds it more than uncomfortable."

"Green jelly? André said something about—oh. I didn't—" Jenny fell silent, her stomach suddenly feeling much like Bob's. She donned her outer clothes, took a fruit from the bag, but then appeared to change her mind about eating. She put it back, thought for a few more seconds, and then spoke.

"What do you want to do now? Do you think a couple of hours rest will get your muscles going again, as it did yesterday? Should we stay here and look over more places after you're back on your feet, or should I help you into the boat and take you back? Do you really think we can accomplish anything here before we have the metal-finder your father was going to get from Mr. Tavaké?"

"We'll stay right here, if it's all right with you. I don't want half the kids on Ell to see me in this state."

"I could take you to the creek mouth near your house."

"I don't want to take the chance. More and more people keep learning about the Hunter, but I don't want it to get to the whole island. I'll keep picking the recruits, and don't want spectators."

"Are you sorry you told me?"

"That's a loaded question, but—no. You know I'm not crazy, and if you're still a little uncertain, your father will straighten you out. I can stand having the word get to people who'll be helpful."

"Then you want to look around Apu some more after you can walk, even if we don't have the detector."

"Right."

"And in the meantime we just wait here and toast." Jenny put no question mark at the end of the sentence, and even the Hunter could see that she had no intention of waiting. He had met numerous human beings who would always be quite willing to sit still and fill a time interval with pointless talk, but he could see that Jenny Seever was not one of them.

She did sit quietly for a little while, thinking, but it was a matter of minutes rather than hours. Then she stood up.

"I'm going to see Mr. Tavaké and find out how long it will take him to make that detector. Your father must have talked to him about it by now. Do you want to wait here until I get back, or shall I take you ashore near your house, or what?"

Bob sat up with an effort. "How are you going to ask him about the detector without starting him wondering what we want it for?"

"Credit me with basic brains, even if I haven't been to an Ivy League college, or whatever they call those places. Your father must have told him something; I don't have to know the reason at all. Are you waiting or coming?"

"I'd better come along. Then if I get back in shape before you show up again, I can do something useful."

"You could search out here."

"Don't rub it in." Bob didn't really like having the initiative taken from him, as the Hunter could well see, but he was not so stupid as to show his resentment. "Let's see if I can get to the boat under my own steam. I know I won't be any help getting it into the water."

"No trouble." Jenny also had some basic tact. She made no effort to help Bob to his feet, though it was plain to her that it was a major struggle. Once up, he walked with less difficulty the thirty or forty yards to the boat. The girl didn't wait for him, and had it in the water by the time he arrived. He got in, still without help. Jenny started paddling, heading for the mouth of the creek nearly two miles away.

After a minute or two, Bob made a suggestion which the Hunter was annoyed with himself for not originating.

"Wouldn't it be smarter if you headed for the nearest part of the shore and then followed it along, in water shallow enough so I can get out fast if I have to? If my stomach acts up again, there's no reason I should mess up your boat."

"Can't you lean over the side?"

"Of course, but is it stable enough? I've been very careful about trim."

"Well, you needn't be. It may not be as stable as an outrigger or a cat, but I've gone in and out in deep water often enough. I told you that. If you need convincing—" Jenny set down the double paddle and, without bothering to remove her outer clothes, startled her two passengers by going overside. The kayak rocked, but not nearly as much as Bob expected; his reflexive grasp of the coaming around the cockpit was superfluous.

A moment later the redhead surfaced. She grasped

the floating hat and handed it to Bob, then seized the coaming and drew herself back aboard. This time the tip was greater, taking the side of the little vessel under water; but the waves still failed to reach the coaming, and the only water which entered the cockpit dripped from Jenny's clothes. She resumed paddling without comment; her passengers also found nothing to say.

She brought the kayak ashore at the mouth of the creek which passed close to Bob's house, far enough up the little stream to be out of sight except to boats well out on the lagoon. Bob managed to get to his feet and disembark with less trouble than he had experienced three quarters of an hour earlier.

"All right," Jenny said. "It will probably be quickest if I go and borrow your bike—it's still at your house, isn't it? You walked down to the boat this morning? Good—and used that to get to Tavaké's phone shack. Do you want to wait here, or get up to the house yourself, or—"

"Hi, Bob! Did you find it?" Daphne's shrill voice cut into Jenny's question, and a moment later the child herself appeared. Bob asked the obvious question.

"What are you doing here, Silly? You don't go swimming alone, especially here away from the beach, and I don't see any of your friends."

"Oh, I saw you coming back long ago in Jenny's boat, and wanted to ask if you'd had any luck. Are you going back out to the little island, or did you find it? If you aren't and still have to look somewhere else, can I go with you? I know Mother won't mind."

Jenny cut in before Bob could answer. "How did you know that Bob was looking for something, Daphne?"

"He said so. That's why Mother said he'd be too busy to have me along."

"Did he tell you what he was looking for?"

"No. It's his secret."

"But still you want to go along? How can you help if you don't know what we're hunting?"

"You're not dressed to go with us," Bob interjected.

"I have my bathing suit on."

"What about the sun, small blonde idiot? We've been looking mostly out on Apu, where there isn't any shade to speak of. That's where you saw us coming from, wasn't it?"

"Then why is Jenny all wet? I can go into the water any time you need, and I don't need sun clothes. I'm tan enough now."

The Hunter was getting impatient. It had been two years since they had been on the island, and even that long ago Bob's sister had been able to hold her own in a verbal duel with anyone but her mother. Bob should have known better than to let this happen; he should simply have said *no*. Unhuman as he was, the Hunter did have emotions, some of them rather similar to those of his human host. He finally yielded to the impatience.

"Which little finger is she wrapping you around this time?" were the words that resonated in Bob's inner ears. He reacted, as the Hunter should have foreseen, with irritation which was taken out on the unfortunate child rather than on the alien critic.

"Look, Silly, Mother told you last night you couldn't come with us, and you can't. We're busy, it's important for us to find this thing, and I can't be distracted looking after you at the same time."

The response did not quite reach the level of tears, perhaps because of the speed with which Jenny cut in. She may have thought Bob was being too harsh, but it is likely that she also wanted to retain some control of the situation.

"Look, Daphne," she said gently and persuasively, "Bob's right about not having you come in the boat with us, but maybe you can help us here on shore. I can't tell you what the thing we're looking for really is, because as you said it's a secret—I don't even know myself; Bob couldn't tell even me." The Hunter

was startled and rather dismayed at this outright falsehood. "I can tell you what it looks like, though, the
way Bob told me. Then you can keep your eyes open
for it and tell us if you ever see it. Remember, though,
it's a secret; you must promise not to tell any of your
friends."

"Sure. How about Mother and Dad?"

"They know already. You can mention it to them
if you like," Bob assured her. The Hunter was not
certain he approved of Bob's tacit acceptance of the
falsehood, but refrained from saying anything to his
host, as the latter went on with the description of the
generator case.

"It's like half a silver ball, about so big." He held
his slightly cupped hands about eight or nine inches
apart. "It's not really shiny like a mirror—more like
our kitchen knives. The flat side is partly covered by
the same silvery stuff, but you can see it's hollow."

"Oh, I know what you mean," Daphne explained
excitedly. "It's mostly grown over with coral, isn't it?"

Jenny did not know what to say, Bob for some
seconds was unable to speak, and the Hunter was not
sure he was hearing correctly.

"It could be," Bob said at last. "You've seen something like that? When were you out on Apu?"

"Never. It isn't there. It's on top of a book case in
the library; it's been there for years."

6. The Moral of a White Lie

The fact that neither Bob nor the Hunter could accept the face value of Daphne's statement carried no weight at all; Jenny was in control. Paying no attention to Bob's expression, which was rather ambiguous anyway, she congratulated Daphne for solving the problem, asked her to lead the way, suggested that they stop at the Kinnaird's to get bicycles, and explained that Bob would have to wait by the boat to meet someone.

The girl's indifference to the truth or falsehood of what she said was bothering the Hunter more and more. The long average life of his species had made it a matter of common knowledge, many generations before, that even the most trivial lie is eventually revealed for what it is; it comes home to roost, because the false information leaves a trail through so many memories.

But Jenny seemed to have no scruples at all about tampering with facts in order to achieve even a short-term end. Worse still, the Hunter's host, while obviously very annoyed, seemed to be more bothered by the girl's assumption of command than by anything else. The feeling of futility which so often drives an immature human being into a temper tantrum was as close to taking over as it ever had been in one of the alien's species. Since Bob was still overcome by his fatigue, neither of them could go with the girls to the library; they could not use the boat, not that there seemed much need to; they couldn't save time by checking up on the metal-finder while Jenny went with Daphne, as she so clearly intended to do—and both Bob and the Hunter were sure they would still need the finder, even for the shield. They did not know what Daphne was talking about, but neither believed it was the real object of their search; though, to make matters even more annoying, they knew they would have to get to the library themselves sooner or later to make certain. In fact, this would have to precede any useful work, since Jenny appeared to be taking Daphne's report entirely uncritically, and would accept nothing less than a direct examination by Bob and the Hunter as grounds for denying it.

All the partners could do was wait, worry, and wonder. Perhaps the worst part was the impossibility of ignoring the chance that the child might be right— which would force extensive replanning.

The library was some two miles away, south of the main road and a little east of where this was joined by the one from the dock. The girls would have to cover the first half mile to Bob's house on foot. Bob wasn't wearing his watch, since it was not waterproof, and they could only guess how long they had been gone. Without saying anything, the Hunter was wondering whether the annoyance would trigger Bob's stomach troubles. That would at least have taken care of the boredom for a while, but he was not really sorry that it failed to happen.

In fact, the girls were back in little more than half an hour, though it naturally seemed much longer. Their voices, well before they arrived, indicated that enthusiasm was still boiling, and Daphne cried out to her brother the moment they came in sight.

"It's still there! Jenny says that must be it! We tried to find out where it came from, but all anyone could tell us was that they thought Maeta had found it before the library was built, and brought it in for decoration when she started working there. She wasn't there today, and wasn't home, we asked as we went by and they said she was out on the water with friends, and she never said where she got it, but we ought to go back and wait for her to come home, and—"

"Throttle back, little one. There are at least four Maetas on the island. I suppose, since you talk about her house being 'on the way,' you mean Charlie Teroa's sister, but I didn't know she worked at the library."

"She does. Also for Dad, sometimes," Jenny affirmed.

"But I still want to see this thing for myself," Bob said firmly, "before I go asking Maeta or anyone else where it came from. Jenny, you never saw the thing we're looking for, and you can't possibly be really sure that this is it." Bob was looking at the older girl as he spoke, but paid no attention to her expression—the eyeballs-rolled-to-the-sky one established by Earth's visual entertainment industry as indicating that something of incredible stupidity has just been uttered. "You went off too fast for me to point that out, Silly. Now I've got to go myself sometime—"

"Well, go ahead," retorted his sister. "We saw André coming away from there, and Jenny said he was the one you were waiting here for. But he wasn't headed this way, so you don't have to wait here. Come on back now."

"What?—Oh, I see—well, I don't—" Bob was completely lost for the moment, and even the Hunter had not expected Jenny's fabrications to come home quite so soon. The redhead covered quickly, however, demonstrating an ability which the Hunter was beginning to feel might not be so desirable after all. Quick wit was one thing, but if its owner used it only for keeping lies more or less up to date it might not be available for more serious matters.

"If André was going toward the dock, Bob and I can meet him with the boat," Jenny said quickly. "You take Bob's bike back home, and then wait for us if you like at the library. We may be pretty late getting there, though, so if you want to do something else, don't wait too long."

"All right." The small brown figure with the almost-white pigtails disappeared up the path without argument. Jenny turned to Bob and the Hunter, but spoke only to the former.

"You get back in the boat. I have something to say to you." Her tone was clearly, even to the Hunter, expressive of extreme annoyance. Nothing else was said until they were afloat and reasonably out of earshot of land; then she went on, "You didn't say anything about these medical problems' affecting your brain. I never saw anyone so slow on the uptake. Do you really want your kid sister chasing around after us on this job?"

"No, of course not."

"Then why didn't you let me convince her that we'd found the thing, and send her off investigating Maeta's past or whatever else might amuse her and keep her out of trouble—and out of our hair?"

"You mean you know that isn't the casing?"

"How would I know? It does fit the description as far as I can tell, but I've never seen the real thing—as you had to go and point out to the kid. Why didn't you go along with my line?"

Bob answered with unusual speed and vehemence.

"Partly because you're right—I'm slow on the uptake. Partly because even if I'd seen what you were up to, or rather been sure of it, I'd still be worried about being around when she learned the truth. I don't want anyone, least of all any of my own family, to be in a position to call me a liar."

"Of course not." Jenny seemed surprised at Bob's seriousness. "Of course no one likes to tell a real lie, but she wouldn't find out until she was older, and you could explain why we'd done it. She'd take it all right. And isn't it important that we get on with this job, without having to baby-sit the kid at the same time? Look, Bob, unless you've been lying too, you're *dying*. This is serious. Are a couple of white lies really more important than that?"

Bob made no answer. The Hunter could have provided him with a full-length speech on the subject, but Jenny's words had forced even him to realize that he hadn't thought of the situation quite that way. He had, after all, been willing to bend regulations in the interest of saving his host's life—though there had been other matters of principle which had helped with the bending—and with a short-lived species such as Bob's perhaps lying wasn't *quite* so serious. He was still unsure of the answer, though not very much inclined to change his long-term attitude, when Bob finally spoke again.

"We'd better head for the library. Do you have a story ready to cover this meeting with André we're supposed to have had—especially if she's met him and mentioned it to him?"

"No, but I'll manage. She's not suspicious, if you mean your sister."

"I do. Not yet." The last two words were pointedly rather bitter, and even Jenny caught their implication. Nothing more was said during the mile and a quarter paddle until near the end, when they saw Daphne waiting for them on the beach by the causeway.

"I suppose you'll tell her it's not the right thing, when you see it." Jenny's tone was more resigned than indignant.

"I'll tell her whether it is or isn't, according to what I see. I appreciate your worry about my health, Jen, but there are some things I can't see doing. I'll kid young Silly in situations we both know aren't serious, and she knows I will, but real out-and-out lying on important matters—no. Maybe I care too much about what she'll think of me after she finds out, but that's the way I feel. Maybe I've been living with the Hunter too long."

"Thanks," the alien muttered.

"Why should she ever have to find out?" asked Jenny, quite seriously.

"Maybe you haven't been living with the Hunter long enough," was Bob's answer. They were ashore by then, and the child was running toward them across the sand.

Bob was not completely restored, but was able to get to the library without letting his condition become obvious to Daphne. Both he and the Hunter were worrying about the other possibility, but nothing more had happened to his stomach since they had left Apu; and now, fortunately, his stomach was practically empty.

The library was a surprisingly large structure, considering the general environment. The reason was another of PFI's policies. Employees' children not only had the option of a college education at company expense, in return for the work contract afterward; the company also covered book expenses, but required that the books come back to the island afterward. Thorvaldsen was not really trying to start a college on Ell, he insisted, but he wanted for both himself and everyone else on the island good access to as much of human culture as possible. It was said that he had once read all the nasty things ever said about capitalists and had set out to prove that none of them had to be true. Whatever his intentions, Ell's population formed a generally well read group, from the relatively few pure-blooded Polynesians, through the mixtures which formed the majority, to the relatively few pure-blooded Europeans. It was also a prosperous population; PFI oil had made the island dependent on the rest of the world for everything but food, but no one was worried; it was likely to be a long time before the oil market failed. Even the foresighted ones who felt that man should shift to nuclear power because of the probable effects of carbon-burning on the planet's climate admitted that PFI was taking as much carbon dioxide from the environment as its customers were putting in.

In any case, the library was large and accessible. It was open, with people on duty, every day from sunrise to three hours after sunset.

The librarian on duty at the moment was a middle-aged woman unknown to the Hunter, though Bob was able to call her by name.

"Hi, Mrs. Moetua. Did my pile of books get here?"

The woman looked up and nodded, without interrupting work on a card she was typing. Then she saw Daphne and glanced toward one of the cases; she was the one who had borne the brunt of the little girl's questioning a short time before, and could guess why the group was there. She swung her gaze back to Daphne, who caught her eye and lowered her voice to a whisper as she led the others toward her discovery.

It was well above eye level even for Bob and Jenny, on top of a case of encyclopedias, and certainly from a distance answered the verbal description which Bob had supplied and his sister modified. It was half hidden by the coral which had grown around it in a complex pattern which fully justified its present use as an ornament.

However, enough of the underlying alloy could be seen to make recognition easy, and Bob and the Hunter looked at it for only a few moments. Neither had any doubt about its identity. The Hunter would have liked to examine it more closely, as a feature he had not noticed in the brief glimpse seven years before now caught his attention, but he decided to wait —Bob was heading back toward the librarian's desk by now, and the alien decided to let him finish whatever he had in mind.

"You told Daphne that Maeta Teroa brought that thing in?"

"I said I thought she did," the woman replied. "That's still the way I remember it. It's been here as long as the building, but so has Maeta, and I'm not absolutely sure. She isn't here today, but shouldn't be hard to find. Why are you interested?"

"I saw something like it years ago out on the reef, and wondered if this might be the same thing. It's certainly curious; I wonder it didn't go out with Museum Exchange."

"They don't get everything," the woman smiled. "Don't make remarks about the Exchange if you want Mae to help you. She does a lot of collecting for them, and we have a lot of stuff here—books and specimens both—as a result."

"Thanks, I'll be careful. I didn't mean to sound critical; I have some minerals at the house which I got from a German museum through that outfit, when I was on my rock-loving bug years ago. I'll ask Mae when I see her; thanks, Mrs. Moetua."

Outside, Bob turned to the girls.

"That saves a lot of time. Silly, I'll have to think of a real prize for you; start making a list of things you want."

"It really is the thing?" Jenny asked.

"It really is—if you can believe me." The young woman had the grace to blush, but kept on with her questions.

"What can we do now?"

"We'll have to get Maeta to tell us as exactly as possible where she found it, so we can try backtracking the way we'd planned."

"What do you mean?" asked Daphne. "Backtracking what?"

"Part of the secret," replied her brother. "Maybe I can tell you later, but I don't promise. You may as well go off and play. There's nothing we can do until I see Maeta, so you won't miss anything. They said she was out on the water?" Both girls nodded affirmatively. "All right. I suppose we could go out in the boat again and try to spot her, but the chances wouldn't be very good—she could be picnicking on any of the islets, even around on the south side, and not just cruising around the lagoon. She could even be fishing or sailing outside the reef."

"But it wouldn't hurt to go see, and you could take me with you in the boat," pointed out Daphne.

Bob looked at Jenny, who smiled and shrugged.

"All right, small sister, *if* you get on your bike, dash home, and put on something sunproof over that scrap of tapa you call a bathing suit. Scoot!" The child vanished.

The rest of the day was spent, not very productively, on the lagoon. Daphne enjoyed herself, and even the older human beings had a good time, but the Hunter was impatient and bored. He could not, in spite of his long life and general tendency toward calm, understand how Bob could apparently put the problem of his own life so casually and completely out of mind. Granted that the trouble was the Hunter's fault, it was *Bob's* life. It did occur to the alien that this might be another consequence of the relatively short human life span; but that could not be the whole story. The Castorian humanoids he knew lived an even shorter time on the average, and he doubted that any of these could have been so casual in such a situation. Certainly none of the individuals he had known personally would have been.

Since most of Ell ate the evening meal shortly after sundown, there was no great difficulty about intercepting Maeta at her home. Daphne had been sent off with the message that her brother would be home a few minutes later; Jenny accompanied him to the home of the Teroas, who lived in the middle of a fairly extensive garden just at the point where the roads met, and only a few score yards from the library.

Bob and Jenny were greeted cordially. Charles, the son of the family, had been one of Bob's close friends for many years. He and his father were at sea just now, as usual, and the older sister was working in the Tahiti office of PFI, but Maeta, her mother, two of the latter's sisters, and a brother-in-law were all there.

More time than Bob would have wished was consumed in answering their questions about his college life—not the sort of questions a Boston or New York provincial would have expected from Polynesians. For once, the Hunter was not bored by human conversation, even though it had no connection with his problem.

It did take a while to steer the talk toward the object in the library, but Bob eventually succeeded. Maeta nodded when he mentioned Daphne's calling attention to it, and admitted, with no particular surprise at the question, that she was the donor of the ornament. When he asked where she had found it she did show a polite curiosity about the reason for his interest, and he told the partial truth that he had used before.

"I thought I saw it in the water years ago, but never tried to collect it," he said. "It was on the outer side of Apu, and I didn't want to be served up as hamburger. You must have had a very calm day, or else you are an awfully good swimmer."

One of the aunts chuckled. "Maeta is a better swimmer and a better sailor than any man on Ell." The girl accepted the compliment with a nod, and Bob remembered hearing something similar from Charles in the past. It was quite believable; her strength was not obvious to the eye, but her coordination was, whenever she moved. Bob did not consciously look at her particularly, but Jenny felt that he was and, to her own surprise, she felt a bit annoyed about it. It would not have been surprising if he had; Maeta Teroa might not have been better looking than Jenny, who had a high and quite justified opinion of her own appearance, but she was at very little disadvantage compared to the much taller redhead. Maeta was just over five feet tall, weighing just over a hundred pounds. Names meant little on Ell as far as ancestry was concerned; she showed her Polynesian background in her brown skin and black hair, but Europe—Scotland, Charles had once mentioned —was visible in her blue eyes and relatively straight nose and pointed chin.

"I won't argue," she said in response to the aunt's compliment. "One doesn't contradict one's elders even to be modest, and I'm not that modest. There really wasn't any risk, though, Bob; I didn't find it on Apu. I spotted it from the *Haerehaere* on the bottom of the

lagoon at least a mile from there—oh, about mid-
way between Tanks Seven and Twelve, as I remember. I was a little surprised to see such a growth
there—it's a species you expect out in the reef—so I
went down to get it. It was pretty, and I didn't let it
go to the Exchange, but kept it at home. When the
new library was finished and I started working there
I took it over—we all helped decorate the place. I've
never figured out how it got so far from the reef. I
thought at first that someone had found it there and
dropped it overboard bringing it in, but I couldn't see
why the person didn't get it back, in that case. It was
in less than twenty feet of water. Besides, you'd think
that any previous owner would have noticed when it
appeared in the library; there can't be many people
on the island who haven't seen it there."

The Hunter put a question to Bob which puzzled
him, but the young man passed it on as his own.

"Did you improve on it any? That is, did you break
off any of the coral to make it look prettier, or is it
just the way you found it?"

"I certainly didn't. I can't see anything pretty about
a broken coral branch, and I remember how glad I
was that all the branches were whole. As far as I know
it's still that way, though I haven't looked closely at it
for a long while. I meant to ask Dad or Charlie what
the piece of machinery inside it might be—I suppose it must have come from some ship—but I never
happened to think of it while they were around. Maybe you know? You were looking at it today."

"I don't know that much about ships, I'm afraid,"
Bob evaded. The Hunter prompted him again. "Would
you come and look at it with me again some time, and
tell me for sure whether it's changed any?"

"Of course." Maeta was clearly puzzled by his interest, but was far too polite to ask for an explanation if Bob didn't volunteer one. "I can't go right now
—we're about to have dinner—but afterward if you
like. You'll stay and eat with us?"

Bob and Jenny made the standard courtesies about

being expected at their homes, and left after agreeing to meet Maeta at the library the next morning. Outside, the Hunter asked why Bob hadn't arranged the examination for that night.

"I doubt they'll really be through eating before the library closes up," he answered, "and I certainly wouldn't want to seem in a hurry to leave the meal, or to hurry them away from it by coming back later."

Jenny, who of course had heard nothing of this exchange, interrupted it by asking Bob the purpose of the questions about the coral.

"I don't know," he had to answer. "The Hunter fed them to me, and I was passing them on for him."

"Without knowing why?"

"There was no way to ask him without being obvious about it. I don't have to speak out loud—he can feel the tension in my vocal cords when I'm not quite speaking—but I'd have had to pause in my other conversation, and people would have noticed."

"Well, why not ask him now?"

"How about it, Hunter?" The alien had no reason to hold back.

"I thought I saw a regularity in the coral arrangement when we were in the library. I'm not sure enough to want to be more explicit until we have another look, and get Maeta's assurance that its present condition either is or isn't the way it was when she first noticed it. Also, I'd like to see if either of you notices anything when you see it next time, so I'd rather not tell you what to look for." Bob relayed this to the girl. Neither was particularly satisfied, and Jenny kept trying to persuade the Hunter to say more all the way to her house. Bob knew better, so the conversation was less strained the rest of the way to his own home.

Predictably, his strength was back to normal when he woke up the next morning. However, a new complication had developed in the form of extreme pain in his joints, especially knees and ankles. As usual, the Hunter could find no specific cause, certainly nothing as clear-cut as the crystals of uric or oxalic acids of gout. The Hunter looked for these with especial care; he had persuaded Bob to take a course in human physiology, and had been very conscientious in doing his host's reading with him.

Presumably one of the plates he was juggling, most probably a hormone, was wabbling in its flight, but the presumption was not very helpful. Bob was extremely uncomfortable physically, but seemed to be getting more philosophical as his condition grew worse. He was quite calm, and showed no signs of blaming the Hunter. The latter, on the other hand, felt himself being driven closer and closer to panic by the combination of guilt and helplessness. He knew that panic could hardly be expected to help, but it attacks on a level far below the reach of intelligence.

Bob was able to move around, however uncomfortably, and ate breakfast with the family without finding it necessary to tell them about the new trouble. Daphne, luckily, had plans to spend the day with friends of her own age, and presented no problem.

Bob and his companion left by bicycle as soon as the meal was over. Nothing had been specifically said about Jenny's being with the party, but she was waiting in front of her house as they passed, and fell in beside them on her own machine for the short remaining distance to the library.

Maeta had not yet arrived, but must have seen them pass her home; they had to wait only two or three minutes for her. They entered the building together, and the smaller woman spoke briefly to the librarian on duty, not Mrs. Moetua this time. Then she led the way to the case on which the coral-encrusted generator housing stood, and gestured to Bob to lift it down—she herself could not reach it. Jenny, for reasons she probably could not have stated clearly herself, reached it first and carried it, still at Maeta's direction, to a table near the door, where sunlight fell directly on it. They all bent over to examine it closely.

There was no doubt in either Bob's or the Hunter's

minds about its being the same object they had seen at Apu years before. This was no longer the main question. Bob and Jenny were trying to see what might have caught the Hunter's notice the day before; Maeta, who had no reason to expect anything special, simply reexamined it with interest.

About a third of the metal surface was exposed, and about as much more was so thinly covered with marine growth that its underlying shape was still plain. From the rest, the limy branches grew in random contortions which even the alien found decorative; the branches were covered with the ribbed cups that had once contained living polyps.

On the bare metal were patterns of fine scratches which were perfectly legible to the Hunter, though only their essential regularity was apparent to the human beings.

The mere fact that the manufacturer's name, serial number, and various sets of mounting and servicing instructions were present was not the peculiarity which had caught the Hunter's attention the day before. Far more surprising to him was the uniformity with which each of these areas of engraving was exposed to view. There were no *partly hidden* words or phrases or numbers. Each symbol or group of symbols was completely free of coral and other growth, as was the metal for several millimeters around it. The coral did not seem to have been *broken* away, but it might possibly have been dissolved.

After waiting for some minutes for his host to notice this, the Hunter posed several leading questions. These also failed to bring Bob's attention to the strange regularity, and the alien finally gave up and pointed it out. Then, of course, it was perfectly clear to the man, and he couldn't understand why he had failed to notice it before.

"Well, you see it now," said his symbiont. "Now let's find out if it was that way when Miss Teroa found it, or if it has become that way since." He left Bob with the problem of executing this simple request.

Logically, the man started with the most general questions possible.

"Mae, are you sure nothing has changed about this thing since you found it?"

"Not perfectly sure, but it definitely hasn't changed very much. Certainly no branches are broken. I admit I don't remember either the exact branch pattern or the arrangement of the patches of bare metal well enough to draw a picture, but if either of these has changed, I don't think it can be very much, either."

"The metal looks the same?"

"As far as I can remember. I'm afraid metal is just metal to me, unless it has a real color like copper or gold."

Bob saw no choice other than to get specific.

"I was wondering about the scratches on the metal. They seem to be only on the bare parts—they never run out of sight under the coral. Of course there may be some scratches entirely under it, but it looks sort of as though someone had been making marks on the steel or whatever it is *after* the coral had grown."

"I see what you mean." Maeta nodded thoughtfully. "I don't remember really noticing the scratches before; maybe someone has been at it. I doubt it, though. The case it's been on is pretty high for young children to reach, and I don't think an adult would spoil it that way." Maeta, like Jenny, had not taken the college option, and for a brief moment Bob was startled by her naïvety. He made no comment, however, even to the Hunter.

They moved around the table, examining the object from all sides. If any bit of the engraving was hidden at all, it was completely hidden, as Bob had said. This, the Hunter felt sure, could not possibly be a matter of chance; and from the near despair of that morning, when Bob had awakened with the joint pains, the Hunter suddenly felt happier than he had in two Earth years. Perhaps that was why he made a mistake.

"Bob," he said. "There can't be any doubt. It can't

be accident. Those areas were uncovered carefully, using acid, to let someone read the engraving, and only my own people could either have expected to find anything to read or have counted on understanding it after it was uncovered!"

It was a forgivable mistake—not the logic, which was perfectly sound, but the failure to see the results of the remark. After all, Bob had seemed to be taking the situation very calmly—unbelievably calmly. If the young man's physical condition had been normal, the Hunter might have been able to spot the emotional tension of his host; but since the alien himself was handling, more or less directly, most of the hormone systems which emotion tends to affect, he had failed to do so. Bob's reaction took both of them by surprise.

"Then they *are* here!" he exclaimed happily—aloud.

Jenny understood, naturally. Maeta, just as naturally, didn't, and was understandably surprised.

"Who is here?" she asked. "You mean you recognize the sort of ship this came from? That doesn't prove anything—I found this years ago, remember."

Bob covered fairly well, but not perfectly. "That's true," he admitted. "I wasn't thinking for the moment. Can you remember *just* when that was? You told us pretty well *where*."

The young woman was silent for some time, the rest watching with varying degrees of patience.

"Let's see," she said slowly at last. "The library was finished early in '51—I remember because I started to work here after school, as soon as it opened, and my first working day was my sixteenth birthday. I'd had this thing quite a while then. A year? No, longer. I never went out in the *Haerehaere* very often—the first time I was only twelve, and that was the year you came home so early and stayed so long, and when Charlie got his first ship job."

Bob nodded encouragingly, but managed to keep quiet this time. The year he had "stayed so long" was the one in which the Hunter's first problem had been solved. Maeta went on.

"It must have been some time in March, either '48 or '49—oh, I remember. I'd been taking care of your sister a lot, and she was walking then, so it must have been March of '49, a little over five years ago."

"Good. Beautiful. Thanks a lot."

"So They, whoever they are, may have been here then, but they don't have to be here now," finished Maeta.

But Bob and the Hunter were sure they knew better.

7. Joke

"Bob, have you time to give us some help?"

The Hunter and his host were both startled. They were still standing around the table which bore the generator case, but there had been several minutes of silence. Everyone had been pursuing his or her own line of thought, some of which had led pretty far from Ell. Maeta's question had not been an interruption, however, since neither Bob nor the Hunter had found a really promising line of thought to follow.

"I guess so," Bob answered. "What is it?"

"Those books you brought back have been brought to the library, and we have to catalog and shelve them. Can you help with the sorting? I'll recognize subjects all right, but we like to have some estimate of scope and difficulty. You've read them—I suppose."

"For the most part," Bob grinned. "All right, I might as well. Jenny, you want to stay and help?"

"No, thanks. I'm not at home in college books, and

might feel lost—at least, I wouldn't be much help. I'll go ask Mr. Tavaké that question we didn't get around to yesterday."

"All right, good idea." Bob read nothing between the lines of her refusal to stay. "Will you be home afterward? I think it's time we talked things over with your father. The next part of the job won't be easy even if Tavaké comes through." Jenny hesitated a moment; the Hunter assumed she had made other plans and was weighing their importance. Bob gave no thought to the pause.

"All right," she finally said. "I'll see you—when? A couple of hours, Mae?"

"The whole job will take days, but that much will get us started," the older girl replied. "If this other thing you're talking about is important, my job can wait—or I can do it all myself, though probably not as accurately."

"We're hung up for the moment on our thing, anyway," Bob assured her. Even the Hunter knew that both Bob and Maeta were merely being polite. He was much less sure about Jenny. Unavoidably, Bob stayed and the redhead departed.

Maeta led the way downstairs. The book crates had been placed beside a large table in a basement room. While it was not regularly used by the library patrons, the walls were lined with partly filled bookshelves. The table was loaded with pots of adhesive, scissors, tape, and similar library equipment, and one corner of the room was occupied by a large, very comfortable-looking armchair with a small table beside it. Maeta looked at these and smiled.

"This was set up as a study for Mr. Thorvaldsen when the library was built, but he fell asleep in the chair so often that he decided to use his old place in the laboratory building. We've taken it over for book processing. How many do you think you have here?"

"Don't remember exactly. They're not all course texts. I was told I could buy other stuff which was recommended to us as reference material; that's why

I can't say I've read every last page of it. I guess the easiest thing is to get it all out on the table and start sorting by subject, unless librarians have some more ingenious way of doing it."

Maeta glanced at him, but had nothing to say to his closing remark, and they started as he had suggested. The girl worked quickly and efficiently, and made good use of Bob's knowledge. She said nothing about the remarks Bob and Jenny had made while they were upstairs, but the Hunter felt sure she was thinking about them. The young woman was obviously far too intelligent not to be curious. The alien was thinking about her more and more as the morning wore on, not only about her evident brains but also about her competence—remarked upon the night before—on and in the water. She could be useful, if Bob's prejudices could be submitted to another blow.

But Bob was getting harder to persuade with each new recruit. It might be necessary to manage Bob for his own good. Jenny would be willing to do that, in principle; but of course there was some difficulty in speaking to Jenny. The Hunter thought deeply, and did not regard the library session as time wasted.

For most of the two hours, Maeta said nothing not directly connected with the job, but just before the session ended she changed the subject briefly.

"Bob, did you say anything to Jenny which could make her think you were laughing at her, or looking down at her, because she hadn't been to college?"

"Not that I can remember. I certainly didn't mean to." Bob's surprise was quite genuine. "What makes you ask?"

"I know she's sensitive about not getting accepted by any college, and something she said when she was leaving a while ago made me wonder whether you'd twisted the knife."

"Well, I never thought about it. I didn't even know she'd applied for a college. Why should staying here bother her? Lots of people don't go—you didn't, and you're older than she is, and it doesn't seem to bother you. Shorty didn't, and it certainly doesn't bother him!"

"Shorty? Oh, the Malmstrom boy." That was an interesting way to put it, since Malmstrom was three years or so older than Maeta. "I don't know much about him. I never applied to a college, and didn't have to face a rejection. I'm perfectly happy here. I like to learn things, and in this library I'd be lifetimes just catching up with what's available. There's just nothing else I want which might take me away from Ell. But Jenny isn't that way, and please be careful what you say to her."

"All right. Thanks for telling me."

Bob took Maeta's admonition at face value, but the Hunter felt there must be something behind it. He tried to puzzle out the possibilities as they went upstairs. Perhaps Maeta felt genuinely protective about Jenny; the redhead was younger, though only by a year or so. She might, on the other hand, be more concerned with Bob and his tendency to be just a little too pleased with his brand new degree, a tendency of which the Hunter was quite aware. He could see no reason why Maeta should be particularly interested in Bob—or rather, while he could see one, he considered it unlikely on such short acquaintance. He had heard it said that females had a general tendency to try to remold any available males, but since the speakers had always been males, he had placed little weight in the claim. He considered it biologically unlikely that there would be major psychological differences between the two human sexes, other than superimposed cultural ones.

He would probably have dismissed the question as both unimportant and insoluble anyway, even if his attention had not been sharply distracted.

Bob had used his bicycle for the mile-and-a-half trip from his house. Maeta had accompanied them to the library door, though she was planning to go back to do more work on the books, and Bob was looking back to utter conventional farewells as he swung aboard his machine. A second later he was sprawled on the concrete.

The Hunter had the damage categorized at once; his host had severe scrapes on the left knee, shoulder, and elbow. He was not quite so quick at deciding how much repair and protection to supply. Had Bob been alone, he would not have lost a drop of blood; but Maeta and the other witnesses who had immediately collected might not be able to believe that anyone could suffer such a fall with no damage. Perhaps the Hunter should allow him to bleed a little—not enough to cause real damage, of course—for the sake of appearances.

On the other hand, the concept of "luck" was widely accepted among human beings, he reflected, and he had noticed that many of the species could dismiss the most incredible events from their minds simply by using this word. The Hunter decided to take the chance. He followed his natural inclinations, sealed off all blood leaks, and got to work on the microorganisms they had picked up.

His partner, surprised though he was, had picked himself up before anyone actually reached him. His first reaction was one of extreme embarrassment, not helped by the words of one of the juvenile witnesses.

"You'd think anyone would look where he was going on a bike, even with a girl around, wouldn't you?"

"I was just—" Bob stopped talking at once, realizing there was nothing he could possibly say which would not furnish more ammunition for a ten-year-old.

"What happened, Bob?" Maeta had returned by now. "Are you hurt?"

"Not physically. My ego will take some repair. I don't really know what happened; the bike just went out from under me." Everyone, including the children who had gathered, clustered more closely to look at the machine. There was nothing obviously wrong until Bob cautiously mounted it again and eased it gently forward. Then it was obvious to all that the handlebars and the front wheel were no longer aligned; with the bar straight across, the wheel pointed noticeably to the right. This would ordinarily have made no difference; a cyclist's reflexes operate off input from the inertial senses and the general visual picture of the terrain. He doesn't keep looking at the front wheel to see where he is going next. In this instance, however, Bob had not really started to roll when he had put his weight on the left pedal and started to swing his right leg across. He had not noticed the change in the handlebar-wheel relationship before he started to move. Naturally he had started a frantic left turn as he began to fall, but the bicycle was moving far too slowly for this to be effective, and with the wheel near ninety degrees, the entire machine had slid from under him, as he had said.

"A smart person keeps his bike tightened up," remarked the youngster who had spoken before.

"Quite right," Bob agreed, paying no more attention to him. "I'm OK, Mae. See you later." He remounted the machine and started down to the road, not looking back this time.

"Shouldn't you tighten it up?" the Hunter asked. "We have tools, don't we?"

"Sure, in the case," was the reply. "It isn't loose, though."

"But—" The Hunter stopped talking as his mind drew too far ahead of his words.

"Yeah. But. We'll think it over later on." There was no time for more conversation, even if there had been thought to feed it. The journey to the Seevers' was short, and they had already arrived.

Jenny met them at the door. If she had been unhappy about anything when she had left them, there was no sign of it now.

"Come on in," she said cheerfully. "Dad's in the office, and we have something to show you." She led the way.

Seever was sitting at his desk, examining with interest an open box about a foot square and half as deep. It was made of thin wood, with the seams heavily caulked and a gasket on the rim where the lid presumably was sealed. Clearly it was meant to be watertight. It contained a quantity of obviously electrical equipment—coils, batteries, and vacuum tubes —which told both the newcomers what it must be, though the details were far from clear. Bob had of course taken several physics courses on his way to the chemical engineering degree, and the Hunter had paid some attention to both reading and lectures, but neither had more than the roughest idea how a metal-detector worked.

"That was a quick job!" Bob exclaimed. Seever answered.

"Not exactly. It was made long ago, well before your father asked for it. Tavaké's kids have been using it for months. The only reason he didn't hand it over when Arthur asked for it yesterday was that the young ones were out using it. Taro was surprised when Jenny came around today asking for the same thing. He only gave it to her when she explained it was the same project and would get to the same people."

"The word's spreading like a tank leak on the lagoon," growled Bob.

"Oh, no," insisted Jenny. "Mr. Tavaké doesn't know what the project is all about. I certainly didn't tell him, and I'm sure your father didn't."

"He certainly knows that something involving several people and his metal-detector is going on. In a place the size of Ell that may not be quite the same as knowing what it is, but it's the same as having everyone know that much—and the identities of the people involved. Well, I suppose it can't be helped. But if we have to ask for anything else, let's have just one person do the asking from now on."

"Did you tell Maeta?" asked Jenny.

"No, of course not. But she has to know there's something funny—"

"Yes, with that slip of yours about 'they must be here.' She probably won't ask me *what* I know, but she'll be asking me whether I know anything. What do I tell her? You were being all pure about lying yesterday, most of the time."

"Tell her the truth, of course," snapped Bob. "That you know, but it isn't your secret." Bob was looking at Jenny as he spoke, and the Hunter regretted not being able to see the doctor's expression. It would have been nice to be able to guess his reaction to the intimation that his daughter was not always truthful. His voice cut in, but by the time Bob looked toward him he was well on his way with another matter, and the expression was probably irrelevant to the earlier question.

"Please let me know what you do tell her, Daughter. Maeta works here sometimes, remember, and I don't want to make any slips talking to her because of what she has or hasn't been told. Personally I think she's a very bright young lady who could be a big help to us, but I understand how Bob feels about letting the word spread any farther."

"I knew it," sighed Bob. "Who else, while you're at it?"

"I wasn't making a serious plea about Maeta, Bob, but I did mention Jenny's mother earlier."

"I thought I'd okayed that."

"You weren't really clear, and I didn't want to take a chance until you were."

"Well, tell her. But let's keep it in the families for a while. Of course, if I get so I can't run things, you're the boss and can do what you think best. Now, how does this metal-detector work?"

"You turn it on here. If the earphones whistle, turn the knob here until it just stops. Then if it comes close to metal, the whistle starts again. If you don't get a whistle at any knob position, put in a new battery. If that doesn't work, take it back to Taro. Nothing to it."

Bob picked up the box. "It's much too light to sink. How do we ballast it for underwater use?"

Seever pointed to a larger box made of concrete, on

the floor beside his desk. What looked like a lid lay next to it. Four eyebolts projected from the sides of the cube, as did an insulated wire; it looked as though the concrete had been poured around these.

Seever's explanation corrected one point; the "lid" was actually the floor of the device. The wooden box was supported well above this, and trapped air would keep any water which leaked in well below the electrical equipment, at least to any reasonable depth, as long as everything was kept upright.

"Taro says it's worked fine for his youngsters," Seever finished. "He's had no trouble with leaks, and they've found a lot of stuff like dropped tools on the bottom around the dock and the tanks. It sounds off for a pair of pliers at five or six feet when it's really at its best.

"Now, Bob, tell me if I have everything straight. Jenny says you are now quite sure that the Hunter's people have been on Earth, and on Ell." Bob nodded emphatically.

"Right," he answered. "They found the generator shield, apparently read its lettering carefully, which the Hunter says would have let them identify his quarry's ship, and for some reason neither of us has been able to guess so far they moved the shield from Apu into the lagoon a mile or so, where Maeta found it. This happened several years ago, but the Hunter is certain they wouldn't have left Earth, at least not for good. They may, he admits, have spread out from the island either to look for him and his quarry because they couldn't find them here, or to check up on the people of Earth, or both. He is certain they would come back from time to time to check on the ship which they probably found, or both of them which they may have found. All we have to do is find at least one of them ourselves and leave a message with it."

"Two questions," Seever spoke slowly, choosing his words very carefully. "First, why would they have moved that shield? It seems to me you're passing over that question very casually, and you admit you haven't an answer. Second, why do you have to find the ships, or one of them, to leave a message? I could see it as a problem when your friends might have been anywhere on Earth, but you now seem sure they're on Ell at least some of the time. Why not paint a message unobtrusively under the dock?"

Bob sighed. "The second answer is the same as it always was. We still have to avoid attracting human attention. A message with any usable detail will be regular and complex enough to get not just attention but real curiosity. Both the Hunter and I feel we can't afford that. For the other point, granted it may be important but we don't see how it can affect our plans. We'd love to figure out the answer, or have someone else come up with a convincing one. Until someone does, we'll have to wonder."

The doctor was silent for at least a minute.

"I still don't like it," he said at last. "I was hoping the Hunter might recognize it as some sort of standard procedure with his police. Maybe it's not important, but I don't like jigsaw puzzles with big gaps in them, especially when there are no pieces lying around. However, we'll have to live with the situation, I guess. You really can't think of a reason, Hunter?"

"I can think of several," the alien relayed through Bob. "It isn't just a matter of police procedure, which is not itself just a matter of following rules. There are dozens or hundreds of situations in which moving the shield would be the obvious thing to do. I was going to do it myself if we had found it on Apu, in an attempt to backtrack to the other ship. Clearly, whoever did it this time was not backtracking."

"Why not?" asked Jenny. "Do you really *know* the other ship didn't land in the lagoon?"

"Of course not," the alien replied, "but backtracking on the comparatively open and smooth lagoon floor would be pointless; from what I've seen, one could go anywhere with equal ease. I was hoping, though not very strongly, that there would be only a few lines of possible travel outside the reef. Anyway, Doctor, I have little doubt that when we do find out why the thing was moved we'll agree it was a good, sound reason, but I don't think I'll be embarrassed for not guessing beforehand what it was. There are just too many good possibilities."

Seever nodded acceptance of the point, and went on talking.

"All right. That leaves us with straight procedure problems. We've made the diagnosis, we have to plan the operation. It seems to consist of hanging this gadget over the side of a boat in all the reasonable places we can think of. These unfortunately include the ocean to the west of the reef, which means we have to keep the machine from getting tangled in bottom coral, and also keep the boat off the reef itself. If you think the crash may have occurred within the reef, I'm completely stumped on what you can do. Bluntly, I very much dislike the idea of taking Jenny's boat outside to windward, and the west side is windward most of the time. You'll have to be careful. I won't forbid it, but I hope you'll use common sense.

"Personally, I'd strongly advise getting a better boat —no reflection on yours, Daughter, but I'd be much happier if you had power available. Since I think it would be silly to trail the detector overside blindly, you should wait for the diving gear that Arthur has ordered; and I'd spend the interval finding a powered craft and arranging to borrow it. You'll also have to try tying your work schedule with those of the people helping you; remember, you won't have as much free time as you like. You do start work shortly, I assume?"

"I'd almost forgotten," Bob admitted. "You haven't come up with any excuse, I take it."

"None that would hold up if you're going to be seen diving several hours a day. Of course, you could take Old Toke into the secret and have him put you to work looking for spaceships."

"We've been through all that. No, thanks."

"Well, we've been through this too, but here it

comes again. I think we're going to need more people to get the job done. Your father and I won't be able to help much, on simple time criteria. Your mother may be free a little more of the day, but she has Daphne to take care of at unpredictable times. I can let Jenny off, of course, to suit the needs of the situation, but neither she nor anyone else should be out there alone."

"She wouldn't be alone. I'll be there."

"And if one of your interesting medical problems rears its head—especially if you're under water?"

"Well—" Bob fell silent.

"Remember, if *I* do the recruiting no one will doubt *your* sanity. I'm willing to let them doubt mine."

"You shouldn't be. You're the only doctor on Ell. If they lose confidence in you, you won't be here long."

"I can prove what I say."

"So could I," retorted Bob, "if anyone would pay attention. The trouble is talking to someone who's walking off shaking his head."

"Have you ever had that happen?"

"No. I'm going by what I'd do myself. Be honest, Doc. When I first told you about the Hunter, what would you have done if you hadn't considered it your medical duty to humor me?" It was Seever's turn to be silent.

"All right," he said at last. "But there are people who would normally humor *me*."

"Your wife, of course," admitted Bob. "But who else?"

"She'll do to start with. In addition, I'd take a chance on the Teroa girl you've already set wondering about you. She's known to be extremely competent in the water. I'll bet she could cover a good deal of the area you want to search, even before the diving equipment arrives."

The Hunter had already considered this point and added his voice to the argument, but Bob was still under the pressure of over seven years' conditioning.

He had not been able to bring himself to veto Seever's request to tell his wife, and had even managed to tell Jenny himself, for reasons which were still not clear to him; but that was as far as he wanted to go for the moment. He didn't phrase it just that way, but both the doctor and the symbiont could see the situation. They gave up for the time being, and the group went back to the logistics problem of planning a way which would give Bob a full day's work without his troubles' being spotted. This seemed to be Seever's business.

"I still haven't found an argument which will get you entirely off work and yet let you go diving, except the one you reject," the doctor said slowly. "I may, though, be able to come up with something which will keep you away from heavy muscle work. There were enough peculiar results in your blood tests to write a good monograph. There is something odd about your calcium. The Hunter isn't doing a perfect job with your sugar. I don't think you'd clot even a pinprick without him, and you don't seem to have any adrenaline at all. He must be doing something or supplying something that does an equivalent job or you'd be pretty dead, but it isn't adrenaline. I can honestly report that your tests are peculiar, *but . . .*" Seever let his voice trail off.

"But PFI might react by sending me to Tahiti, or even to Japan or the States, for more checkups and treatment."

"Exactly."

"Can't you tell them just a little? That the tests seem funny and you want to make sure, and I should be kept at desk work or something so you can get at me whenever you want during the day? If I'm not doing heavy work I might either avoid the fatigue or be able to hide it, and I can cover up the joint pains well enough."

"That's all I can see our doing for now," Seever agreed. "I'll write it up that way, and you report for work tomorrow and see what happens. We may as well try it this way. I don't see what else we can work on until the diving gear comes, since you won't let Maeta in on the operation."

"I'm not quite sure about that." Jenny spoke up for the first time since the medical questions had come up. Both men looked at her inquiringly, and her father asked for clarification.

"You mean we can do something to get the equipment here sooner? Or do you know of some here already?"

"Neither. I think I have an idea about getting something done before the diving stuff arrives at all. I'm not really sure, and I want to think it over. Bob, if you'll come here tomorrow after work—you'll want to anyway, so Dad can see how you're doing—I think maybe I can come up with something that will bypass the diving equipment for a while. All right?"

"You're sure you don't want to tell us now?" asked Bob. "It could save a day, you know."

"I'm sure I don't, because I'm not sure I'm right. I don't want to look silly." Bob looked at her father, who shrugged.

"I guess that adjourns the meeting," he said. "Bob, you go home and get as many hours sleep as you possibly can. Hunter, there's nothing I can tell you to do. Jenny, work your think box, and if I can help any way without butting into your secret, tell me. One other thing, Bob; drop by on your way *to* work in the morning and pick up my report on you. I'll do my best, but don't expect too much. Old Toke has always had the idea that recent graduates should be impressed as quickly as possible with the fact that they're not really indispensable, or even very important."

The meeting broke up. Bob went home without any attempt to adjust his bicycle, and he was late getting the rest Seever had recommended because Daphne was on hand.

After she went to bed he updated his parents on progress, but omitted any mention of the bicycle incident.

The Hunter spent the night on biochemical work which might or might not have been useful; Bob did not have the joint pains in the morning. Seever's report apparently accomplished something, for the Hunter and his host spent the day in the refinery watching dials and turning valves. The work wasn't too hard. Bob's muscles held out to get him back to the doctor's in the late afternoon.

And Jenny's idea was of the sort one kicks one's self for not thinking of earlier.

8. Routine, Modified

It may not have been completely safe, but for the Hunter it was quite comfortable. A foot-and-a-half length of three-inch pipe had been secured with wire to one side of the concrete outer case of the metal-detector. A wooden plug closed the upper end of the pipe. The inner side of the plug held a small improvised electric switch, which closed the circuit in a two-strand wire leading up along the rope which supported everything. The Hunter could send buzzer signals to those above, though they had no direct communication with him so far.

The bottom of the pipe was open, allowing the alien to look down with an eye composed of his own tissue. It was planned to make an artificial one for him from a lens and a short cylinder of opaque material, but this had not yet been completed. It would have advantages; the Hunter's flesh was not completely transparent, so that it did not make a particularly good lens, and was not completely opaque so that his "eye" did not exclude stray light really well. He could see, but generally preferred other eyes to his own.

The bottom was very irregular, and the coral growing from it was even more so, so he had to keep sending "up" and "down" signals to the people above. The most inconvenient part of the setup was the fact that the phones of the detector were also up in the boat, and there was no convenient way for Bob and Jenny to let the Hunter know when the device responded. They had tried tying a string to a washer held in the Hunter's tissue inside the pipe, but there were so many spurious signals from the boat's own motion that this had been given up. Bob had suggested a flashlight bulb in the pipe, operated by a key in the boat through a separate circuit, but this had not yet been built.

Over a week had passed since Jenny's suggestion had been made. Between work and weather, very few hours had been spent in actual search. The vague beginnings of a map of the sea's bottom beyond the reef existed, but filled a very small fraction of the master sheet which Arthur Kinnaird had made from the company map of the reef itself.

Checking the position of the boat every minute or two in order to keep track of the area which had been covered was a major nuisance, even though a brainstorming session in which all had participated one evening had resulted in a fairly rapid fix technique based on horizontal angles measured between corners of selected pairs of the tanks in the lagoon. The Hunter would buzz a number whenever he saw a fairly distinctive feature, and note its details with a piece of pencil graphite on a sheet of paper lining the pipe; at the sound of the buzz, those in the boat would measure and record position. During the evenings of days when they managed to work at all, the Hunter and Bob would correlate the sets of records and make the appropriate additions to the main chart.

There was a good deal of metal on the bottom; human beings seemed to have a tendency to lose things overboard. So far, all the specimens had been too small to give signals which could possibly be from a spaceship, except for one which had been found the first hour of operation. Checking it out had been long and complicated; the word had not reached the Hunter until the kayak had pulled into North Beach for rest and lunch. Afterward the site had to be found again, and the Hunter lowered to the bottom so that he could extend a pseudopod into the mud to analyze the object. It had proved to be a well-rusted, extremely large anchor. All the Hunter could do was buzz "no" to his crew. When he gave them the details later, they guessed it had been lost from a sailing ship at least a century before, possibly while trying to hold off the reef during a storm.

Procedures were gradually improved as the days went on, but the charted area increased with painful slowness. There was no real danger, though the Hunter was constantly beset by very small fish and arthropods. Biochemically his tissues were Earthlike enough to be digestible by Earth organisms, and conversely; it was something of a race every hour he was in the water to see who ate more of whom. Because of the protection of the pipe, the Hunter was able to keep ahead, but he realized how lucky he had been to meet and occupy the shark so soon after his crash beside the island.

For Bob, the days were not going very badly; fate seemed to be holding its fire for the moment. He had not suffered the strange fatigue for nearly two weeks, whether because of or in spite of Seever's and the Hunter's combined efforts there was no way to tell. To forestall any complacency, the weariness had been replaced by the joint pains in more serious form, and, in the last few days, by muscle aches and cramps. The latter were usually in the legs and waist, and sometimes he was finding it difficult to conceal them from his fellow workers; they struck suddenly and without warning. Malmstrom, whom he saw at times, made occasional remarks about his old friend's deteriorated condition, but didn't seem to mean them too seriously so far.

The PFI work had been a nuisance mostly because of the time it demanded. Bob liked it well enough for its own sake, and even the Hunter was interested. Jenny had suggested that she take the Hunter out during Bob's work hours, accompanied either by her own mother, or Bob's, but the Hunter had firmly vetoed this. It was bad enough, from the alien's viewpoint, to leave his host for a few hours at a time even when they remained near each other and could rejoin on a few minutes' notice. If they were apart by the three or four miles which separated the search area from the refinery, he would not even know if he was needed for perhaps hours.

About the fifth day of actual search—as Seever had predicted, wind permitted their operation much less than half the time, and they had met with no success in borrowing a powered craft—a problem which no one had seriously considered developed, to show that any separation at all of host and symbiont could lead to trouble.

It was about half an hour before sunset. The Hunter had been rather pitying the boring time his young friends must be having, in contrast to his own, when the situation changed abruptly.

The Hunter was several seconds realizing what had happened. The motions of the boat were always providing some vertical acceleration, and no shock or blow accompanied the parting of the rope. It just quietly let go, and the detector and the Hunter were on their way to the bottom. There was a slight jolt as the wire took the load. This, surprisingly, held, jerking the wooden plug out of the top of the pipe and taking the switch and almost taking some of the alien's tissue with it. By the time he had recovered from this surprise, he and the detector were half buried in limy mud.

Three and a half fathoms above, consternation

reigned. Bob had been holding the rope while Jenny
held position with the paddle, but she knew almost as
soon as he did what had happened. Small as the load
was, its disappearance had altered the trim of the
kayak, and the girl knew her craft very well indeed.

"Did you drop him? Have your muscles quit
again?" she asked anxiously.

"No. The rope seems to have broken or come un-
tied. If I'd lost my hold we'd still have him; I had it
snubbed on a cleat."

"Take the paddle, and hold us here!" the girl
snapped. He turned to see that she was already strip-
ping down to her bathing suit.

"No! Wait!" he said. "Make sure we know what the
position is, first!" He snatched the sextant, made quick
readings on the reference tanks, and wrote them
down. Then he started to remove his own shirt, re-
marking as he did so, "We ought to have had some
sort of emergency buoy that we could throw over to
mark the spot when something like this happens."

"What are you doing? You can't go down!" snapped
Jenny. "You're not even as good a swimmer as I am
when you're in good health, let alone now."

"And I'm not as good a paddler, and if you do go
down and find the other end of the rope somewhere on
the bottom, what are the chances of my keeping the
upper end in your reach?"

"Do your best. Give me the free end, pay out all
the slack you have, and take the paddle." Bob followed instructions, not because he was convinced she
was right but because it seemed a poor time to argue,
and Jenny disappeared overboard.

The Hunter could see the canoe, and saw the girl
enter the water. Neither view was very encouraging.
The kayak had already drifted at least twenty yards
from his position, and Jenny, while apparently going
as nearly straight down as she could, seemed unlikely
to get anywhere near him. Indeed, she did not even
reach the bottom; with a fathom still to go, her descent
slowed and stopped. She drifted for a moment, evi-

dently trying to see, but her natural buoyancy took over, and after a few seconds she began assisting it.

Her head broke the surface a dozen feet from the kayak. Bob, forgetting for the moment the importance of trying to hold position, paddled over to her while she was getting her breath.

"Any luck?" he asked. She climbed back aboard before answering.

"No. I couldn't quite get to the bottom. We should have goggles; I couldn't see clearly enough to spot the box and pipe, to say nothing of the rope. The sun will be down soon, too. There isn't a chance of finding him tonight. We'll go in, and you get in touch with people and arrange enough time-swapping at the refinery so you can spend all day tomorrow out here."

"I don't like to leave—"

"I don't either, but it's a case of what we can do, not what we want to do."

"But the Hunter could leave the pipe and swim to the boat, if we wait long enough."

"Fighting off all the small fish and animals he's been telling about? He's too smart to try, I'd think. Could he find us in the dark?"

"I don't suppose so. His eyes aren't too good."

"Well, we'll compromise. We'll stay as close to the spot as we can until sunset. If he hasn't shown up by that time—and I still don't think he's dumb enough to try because he'll know we can find the instrument more easily than anything else—we'll go in, and you'll do what I told you."

"All right. What will you do?"

"Go home and report to Dad, make a couple of marker buoys as you were suggesting, and think."

She did not mention that she had already been thinking, and fully intended to do something else.

The Hunter watched the boat hopefully until the light failed, rather wondering why no one dived again and what was going on up above. Jenny was quite right on one point; he did not consider for a moment leaving the shelter of the pipe and trying to swim to the kayak. He waited. When the light faded and he could no longer see the surface, the boat, or anything else but a few luminous life forms, he continued to wait. There seemed nothing else to do but think, and he had to do that anyway.

Jenny and Bob left the kayak at North Beach, the point at the end of Ell's longer arm, where the Hunter had come ashore and found Bob nearly eight years before. Their bicycles were there, since they had been using this as a staging area from the beginning in order to save time, but there was no moon and no easy way of keeping the machines on the road, so they were some time getting even as far as Bob's house. He stayed there very briefly, telling his mother that they were off the water but that he had to get to a telephone, and went on to fulfill the assignment which Jenny had given him.

The girl herself had not stopped. She went on to the Teroa home and asked to see Maeta. The latter turned out to be at the library. Jenny went there, found the other girl downstairs working on new books—Bob's were not the only cratefuls to reach Ell each June—asked her to come outside where they would not be overheard, and told her the whole story.

Maeta had of course been wondering about the things Bob had said in his unguarded moment, but this did not make Jenny's tale any easier to believe. Jenny was both insistent and persuasive, however, and the older girl eventually agreed to go to the Seever house. There, the report of the Hunter's loss produced such obviously genuine concern on the part of the doctor and his wife that Maeta's skepticism weakened. Seever added verbal assurance of the truth of the whole story, with details from the old detective adventure which Jenny had not known. Finally, still with some reservations, Maeta agreed to offer her aquatic skill to help in the recovery of the equipment and, if he existed, of the Hunter. She also agreed to furnish her own outrigger, a more stable and capacious craft than the kayak. Since she was not on duty at the library the next day, there would not be the problem of finding a substitute.

When Maeta had left, Seever looked quizzically at his daughter, and asked, "What excuse are you going to make to Bob for this piece of recruiting?"

"If he thinks excuses are needed, his brain really is getting soft. If he doesn't like it, he can just stew. Are you suggesting that you don't like it, either?"

"On the contrary," her father assured her. "It was the smartest thing you could have done. I'm not sure I'd have had the—er—force of personality needed to do it, that's all. Bob is not entirely out of order, feeling the way he does."

Jenny refused to pursue the subject.

"Do we have any good, strong twine here, or will I have to go to the store in the morning?" she asked. "I've got to make some marker buoys."

The Hunter spent a night which would have been fascinating to a marine biologist specializing in crustacea. He did not come dangerously close to being eaten, as the pipe provided more than enough physical protection, but he himself had to do a certain amount of eating, largely in self-defense. He observed interesting details of structure and physiology in the creatures he digested. It was the relatively coarse features, down to about optical microscope limits, which proved most deserving of attention; at the molecular level the things were essentially the same as Bob and his father and, presumably, the rest of Earth's metazoan life.

A marine biologist might have been annoyed to see a boat coming, but the Hunter was vastly relieved. Even when it was close enough for him to see that it was not the same boat, he had no doubt that it was coming for him. He was very concerned about his host's condition. They now had been apart for nearly fifteen hours. This would have been unimportant a few years ago, but it might very well be crucial by now. He watched anxiously.

He could see the outrigger, and could see that the craft was driven by three paddles. These slowed their motion as it approached; one was withdrawn, and the canoe came to a near halt ten or twelve yards from directly overhead. It held position very well for a minute or so. Then something splashed into the water. For a moment the Hunter thought it was a diver; then he realized that it was a rock or a lump of coral. Presumably it was serving as an anchor, though his improvised eye was not good enough to see any line attached to it.

Then a second object splashed through the ripply surface. This one was smaller still, and it took much longer for him to realize that it was simply a buoy, in the form of a short, brightly painted stick connected to another piece of rock by an even thinner cord. Before he had fully worked this out, a third object had entered the water.

This one made much less splash than either of the others. The Hunter was able to recognize a human figure, but not to identify it. This time the diver displayed no difficulty in reaching the bottom, and swam in widening circles for fully half a minute before shooting to the surface for air. At one point, she was close enough to the Hunter to let him see her clearly, and he was pleased to recognize the Teroa girl. He remembered what had been said about her skill in the water, and felt that he was as good as rescued.

On her second dive he was not so sure. She stayed down almost as long, and covered almost as large an area of sea bottom, but she was obviously working away from his location.

Presumably she would come back sooner or later, but there was no way of guessing which. There was also no way of guessing Bob's condition, and the Hunter was once again coming as close to panic as his species could.

He wondered how far the girl could see things clearly; he himself could not tell whether she was wearing goggles, though it seemed likely. He hoped so, since human eyes focused so poorly under water. There was nothing he could do about her eyesight, but could he improve the visibility of the tank, or the pipe, or the rope? Failing that, could he do anything to shift the search pattern in his direction?

The lump of coral anchoring the marker buoy was probably movable, but was over ten yards away. Leaving the pipe and traveling to it through the mud would be unpleasant and perhaps risky, but that was irrelevant; the only question was whether he could move the anchor when he got there.

He knew that with this idea formulated, he would probably not be able to come up with another until he had at least tried it. This was a characteristic he had also noted in human beings. There was nothing to do, therefore, but try it.

He had covered three quarters of the distance when another idea did strike him, but by then it seemed better to go on. He finally reached the rock.

It turned out to be one of those annoying in-between things, light enough so that he *could* lift it, heavy enough to make actual transportation a major project. He spent some time at it, moved it a foot or so, and finally decided that this would take too long. He went back to his pipe and began to implement the second idea.

The hardest part of this was to get the trapped air out of the concrete box, and hold onto it afterward. He could ooze through the space between lid and box easily enough, though it was supposed to be watertight. Since the gasket had indeed held, the pressure was lower inside, and forcing microscopic bubbles of air against the gradient involved more work—in the literal sense in which the physicist uses the word—than he had counted on. Also, when the volume of gas he had collected began to grow large, he could no longer keep both it and himself inside the pipe. Outside, he had to devote some of his attention to the Hunter-eating zooplankton.

At the same time, he was slowly drawing the broken rope toward himself, until he had the end in reach.

He stopped taking air when the water, which he had had to allow into the box to bring the pressure difference down to something he could handle, came close to the electrical equipment. Wetting this would probably cause even further delay, and the bubble seemed big enough.

Maeta had stopped twice to rest during all this, but was now working far enough away to cause the Hunter to worry whether even this idea would be good enough. There seemed nothing else to do, however, so when she started down the next time, he released his hold on pipe and box and let his air bubble carry him and the rope upward.

The lifting power of the air proved sufficient for the whole length of the rope, so he came to rest about half way to the surface. The sun was not yet very high—the outrigger had arrived very shortly after sunrise—but the waves were high enough to refract its beams downward at regular and frequent intervals—probably better, the Hunter felt, than uninterrupted light. He kept the walls of his bubble as thin as tactical necessity permitted, and waited. He also wondered whether Bob remembered the item about total internal reflection which they had both read in an elementary physics course.

The flashing reflection from the bubble naturally caught Maeta's eye, though she was more than twenty yards away. She swam over to investigate, since it hadn't been there before and was certainly something unusual. The Hunter saw with satisfaction that she was wearing goggles, and it was obvious that she saw the rope, though what she made of him and his bubble he could not guess. She followed the rope to the bottom, and saw and recognized the equipment.

She returned to the surface for air, then came down again and walked the marker buoy over to the site. While she took her next rest, the Hunter released his air and settled to the bottom; and before the new line was bent on, he was safely back in his pipe.

9. Joke Two

Rather to the Hunter's surprise, neither Jenny nor Maeta showed any revulsion at the sight of his greenish jelly soaking into the hand Bob dipped into the open top of the pipe. They watched only briefly, not because of their own feelings but because the alien could not stand the sun for long.

Maeta offered to stay with them for the day and continue the regular search, but the Hunter wanted to stay with Bob long enough to make a complete check for all the things which might have gone wrong in his absence. This meant that a diver would have to spend most of her time keeping the instrument out of the coral, and this seemed impractical until the Cousteau equipment arrived; and no one yet knew when that would be. Seever, the third paddler, also had a point to make.

"You've been more in the water than out of it for the last hour and more, Mae. I know you don't feel either cold or tired, but take care of yourself. Get some rest before you go in again." The girl laughed.

"I could stay in all day. I have, sometimes," she pointed out, looking back at the doctor without interrupting the rhythm of her paddle. "I not only don't *feel* tired; I'm really not."

"Ordinarily I'd agree with you, young lady," Seever answered, "but this time you've spent a lot of time under water. I know you've trained for that, too, and are probably in better condition than anyone else on Ell for such things—yes, I know all about your reputation; who doesn't? Still, there are things no human body can put up with indefinitely. You take care of that one."

Maeta laughed. "Aren't you going to tell me to put something on to keep the sun off, over this bathing suit?"

"No. I'm a professional trying to do his job, not an old fogey asking to look ridiculous. If my daughter or Bob were dressed as you are, I'd have jumped on them already. I know as well as you do that you don't need it. Are you trying to get compliments out of a middle-aged man? There must be better directions to shoot."

Maeta said nothing, nor did Jenny, but the latter looked at her father as teen-agers have been looking at their parents for generations. Bob paid no attention; he was listening to the Hunter's generally favorable report on his own condition, and promising himself that a very careful check of ropes, wires, and other equipment would precede any future operations.

The rope which had failed had been examined closely by everyone. Jenny had suggested openly that Malmstrom had done something to it. Bob had countered with the suggestion that it was the "pest" André desChenes. The rope itself failed to support either contention; it had not been cut, quite certainly. There was no obvious reason why it had failed, and the rather futile argument was still going on when they reached North Beach.

"When the Hunter finishes his checkup, I'd like very much to go back out," Maeta said when the outrigger had been pulled up. "I like being on the water, and this is as good an excuse as anyone could have— not that anyone needs an excuse. I wouldn't have to do enough diving to bother you, Doctor, judging by the number of times they've found large pieces of metal. There's room for me in your kayak if you'd rather use that; I admit it's a lot lighter."

Jenny's feelings were mixed. The search itself was getting boring, except when she remembered what it meant to Bob. Even then it was beginning to be duty rather than pleasure. Also, she was beginning to change her mind, for reasons she couldn't have given even to herself, about the wisdom of having Maeta in the group.

Bob thought the idea was excellent, however, and the Hunter also voted in favor of it; so the group headed for the kayak, with Seever and Maeta carrying the concrete-and-pipe assembly. The remains of the other coil of rope, which had failed the day before, still lay on one of the duckboards in the kayak's bottom, and Jenny picked this up and tossed it out on the sand. Then she gave an exclamation. "Hey! Look at this!"

The others, gathering beside her, had no trouble seeing what she meant. At the side of the duckboard, where it came closest to the canvas but had been hidden by the rope, both the wood and the canvas were deeply stained. Jenny touched the canvas, and cried out again as the brown-tinted portion, nearly three inches across, crumbled away.

Her father bent over and sniffed.

"Nothing I can tell now," he said, "but it looks like acid—battery acid, for a guess."

"That punk Shorty!" snapped Jenny.

"Or André?" queried Bob.

"Why him?" asked the redhead. "He's asked me if he could come out with us, and I said yes, in a few days."

"Maybe the few days got too many. I can't see Shorty doing anything as serious as this; he's more the chalk-in-the-blackboard-eraser type."

"I suppose the acid was poured on the rope, and the bit that got on the canvas was accidental," Seever said slowly. "I can't see why it was done at all, though I'm afraid I agree with Bob that it's something André might do."

"It's certainly a serious question," Maeta agreed, "but there's another. Are you going to let this hold up the real project? Isn't it still important to find those ships if we can? Or do you want to wait until the diving equipment gets here, if it ever does?"

"Things will go so much faster with it that I'd almost just as soon wait," Bob admitted. "We're spending an awful lot of time and effort to cover an awfully tiny patch of map. Maybe I'll last until the breathing stuff gets here—"

"And maybe you won't," snapped Jenny. "Mae's right. We've got to keep this going."

"We can use my rigger until your kayak is fixed," Maeta added. "After that, too, if you want. The rest of my family won't mind—and I don't have to tell them what we're doing, Bob." The Hunter was impressed; he hadn't known that the small girl had been so aware of Bob's feelings. Had she been reading his host's expression that well, or had Jenny told her? Maeta was continuing with her ideas. "Look, I don't work at the library every day. Jen, you and I can do some of the job while Bob is working at the refinery—"

Bob cut in with the Hunter's objection to being so far separated from his host. Maeta waved it away.

"He won't have to be," she said. "We won't need the Hunter. I can go down to check how far off the bottom the box is every few minutes, and we can make position work easier by using a lot of those marker buoys. We can make more of them easily. We'll fill that map three or four times as fast as you're doing it now. Come on, we'll start right now. I suppose you don't want to come, Doctor; Bob's all right now, and you don't like to spend too much time away from your office. But come along if you like, of course; there's plenty of room in the rigger."

The Hunter, who had seen comparatively little of human females during Bob's college career, was beginning to wonder whether the tendency to take control of things was universal among them, or merely half-universal among human beings. Many of Bob's male friends at college had been pretty bossy, too, the alien reflected.

"Thanks, I'll go back to the office," Seever answered, "but you take care of yourself out there, Mae. You're probably safe from sunburn and coronary, but there are other things under the water, and you'll be alone." Maeta's face lost its expression of rather pixyish humor, and she looked Seever soberly in the eye.

"I know, Doctor. I'll be careful—really." She turned to the others. "Let's go."

The next day or two went well, except for Bob's condition; joint and muscle pains were growing much worse, and neither Seever nor the Hunter was able to do anything about them. The neostigmine Seever had sent for seemed to palliate the weakness, which had not been experienced for some time, and the nausea attacks also seemed to have vanished. Both the human and nonhuman experimenters would have liked to take credit for the latter, but neither dared to; neither was sure it wouldn't come back.

The weather permitted the girls to work outside the reef, and a very encouraging amount of area was added to the Hunter's map from their reports.

The Hunter himself was shocked to find that he had mixed feelings about this. He would have been happier to be on the spot himself. Now he found that he was spending much of his host's sleeping time wondering what they would do when the entire planned area had been covered without success. Should they expand the area, or go over the whole thing again? Which would give the better chance? There had been little more than guesswork available to establish the area in the first place, but it had seemed such reasonable guesswork!

He sometimes asked these questions of Bob, but had little profit from it. The young man was either in one of his philosophical moods, and merely answered that they could face those difficulties when and if they arose, or was irritated and would threaten to calm them both with alcohol if the Hunter didn't stop bothering him. The alien did not really believe the threat, but had learned to be uneasy about human beings who had talked themselves too loudly into a corner.

The real, major hitch in the general operation occurred five days after the Hunter was fished from the bottom. It was not only a Sunday but also a major holiday—the Fourth of July—which made some difference in the regular work pattern. The refinery operated, of course, but Bob did not have to report until midmorning. His father had left the house quite early, Daphne and her mother went a little later to join most of Ell's holidaying population on the beach and dock, and Bob had remained late in bed. He got his own breakfast with little time to spare, and headed down toward the road on his bicycle. His joints were a little less bothersome than usual, but still made motion uncomfortable.

The Kinnaird house was slightly more than two hundred feet from the main road. This end of the island was heavily overgrown with the thorny byproducts of PFI's early efforts to breed fast-growing material for the culture tanks. The driveway was not perfectly straight, so it was impossible for Bob to see far ahead. It was also, fortunately, impossible for him to ride very fast.

The machine was almost to the final turn, ten or fifteen yards from the main road, when it stopped. Bob didn't. He gave a startled yell as he went over the handlebars, but that was all his reflexes accomplished. The Hunter's provided the usual tightening up around joints to help in sprain defense. Neither response proved really useful.

The driveway was not paved—it was really little more than a path, though a jeep could negotiate it. On the other hand, it was far from soft. It was met first by Bob's left hand, followed closely by shoulder and head on the same side. Both forearm bones snapped, the flesh on the left side of his cheek was badly torn, and his left ear was almost removed. The Hunter had plenty to do, but this did not include anesthesia; his host was thoroughly knocked out.

At first the alien was not aware of anyone else in the neighborhood, and could do his normal job without worrying about the need for camouflage. He promptly blocked the opened capillaries, and the larger vessels where bone had come through the skin; practically no blood escaped. He was working the displaced face and head tissue back to its approximately correct place when he heard something.

At first he could not decide its nature; then it began to resemble a fairly large body making its way through the underbrush. Presently this ceased, and very faint footsteps sounded on the drive. The Hunter was relieved at first; getting Bob to the doctor's place was obviously necessary, and obviously more than the symbiont could manage unaided. Whoever was coming should be able either to give help or go for it. Bob's eyes were closed, so his partner could see nothing even though they had come to rest lying flat on his back.

The alien tried to force one lid open to see who was standing over them, but had not succeeded when a thin sliver of metal went through his host's chest, nailing him neatly to the ground. The Hunter forgot all about seeing, and barely noticed the fleeing footsteps. He was suddenly very busy.

The metal had entered Bob's body at the base of the breastbone and slanted a trifle upward, going through the right ventricle of his heart and emerging just to the right of his spine. The heart continued to beat on its own, but the symbiont had to surround it with his own tissue to prevent blood from escaping through the two holes and filling the pericardium, which would seriously hamper *heart* action. The metal helped plug the holes, but was doing no good otherwise. For the moment, all the Hunter could do was maintain blood pressure and circulation until help showed up. There was no immediate likelihood that it would.

Bob came back to consciousness in fifteen minutes or so. The Hunter recognized the fact before his host started to move, and told him slowly and carefully what was wrong, to prevent his doing so incautiously. Bob listened, and finally understood.

"What can we do?" he asked. "I know you can keep me alive, but I'd hate to have the family find me this way."

"I agree, though probably not for the same reasons," the Hunter answered. "The average human being who saw you might react by pulling out this piece of metal, and that's something I want done only under my guidance or Dr. Seever's. Do you think you're strong enough yet? Don't worry about shock; I'll handle your blood pressure."

"I guess so." Bob reached carefully toward his chest, and felt the projecting end of the weapon. "I'd say this was one of those picnic skewers we cooked with the other night."

"That was my impression," responded the alien, "though I've only felt the part inside you. Fortunately it's one of the straight ones, not the twisted kind. I'd have missed more of your blood otherwise, there'd have been a lot more damage to your heart, and you'd be having a much tougher job of pulling. Get hold of it—there—and work it very slowly upward. I'll take care of the inside. That's good—that's right—very slowly, especially when the point comes out of the ground—you don't want it to wiggle any more than we can help—that's the way—"

The Hunter kept talking. Some time Bob was going to become fully aware of what he was doing, but that moment should be postponed if at all possible until the skewer was out of him, or at least out of his heart. If nausea, a very likely result of full realization, were to occur before then, the Hunter would have a distinctly more complex job. He made it a point to hold his host's eyes closed; for even though he was not permitting any blood to emerge with the metal, the sight of the thing protruding from one's own chest was something to be avoided. The Hunter could regard

the operation with professional interest; Bob was unlikely to possess quite that much detachment.

It took several minutes, but they managed it without doing any more damage. In spite of the fluid pressure and constant motion, the Hunter had no trouble
holding the heart punctures closed; he judged they
would heal in a few days, barring fallout from the
other problems, and told his host so. "But in the meantime, don't do anything which might raise your blood
pressure too much," he finished.

"Does that include standing up and walking?" Bob
asked. "It seems to me I should get to the doc without waiting for someone to come home. Now that
you're letting me look at things, I get the impression
that someone ought to set this arm. Thanks for taking care of the sensation, by the way."

"Well, for once it wasn't your own carelessness,"
his companion replied. "I'm not strong enough to set
your bones. Let's see what caused this fall, and then
we'll walk, very slowly, to the doctor's."

The Hunter by this time had checked all his host's
injuries. The blow which had knocked him unconscious seemed to have produced no real brain
damage. His skull was intact, and while the Hunter
never dared intrude in actual brain tissue except
within the blood vessels of that organ, none of these
seemed damaged and there had been no leakage of
blood into the cerebrospinal fluid.

Bob found movement no more painful than before,
and made his way to the bicycle. What had happened
was fairly clear.

The front tire was cut to the rim; nothing else was
visibly wrong. Bob summarized.

"Someone stretched a wire across the road about
hub high. After I went into it, he removed the wire
and skewered me, not necessarily in that order. That's
clear enough. But I don't see why; it seems a little
extreme for one of André's practical jokes—not the
trip-wire, but the stabbing, wouldn't you say?"

The Hunter had to agree, though he had thought of the same child himself.

They could find no trace of where the wire had been attached, though there was no lack of possible places. The Hunter wondered whether any eleven-year-old could have hidden his tracks so well, but kept the thought to himself. He could reach no conclusions except that someone was not very concerned with Bob's health—there was no way of being sure that the offender even had anything particular against the young engineer; he might have been merely a target of opportunity. The alien had not practiced his profession for several years, and began to wonder whether he was losing the touch. He should, he felt, have been sure of *something*.

Bob insisted, over his partner's objections, on wheeling the bicycle back to its shed before heading toward the Seever home-cum-hospital.

"If the folks come back before I do and find it in that shape, they'll go crazy," he pointed out. "You can just keep my heart plugged up a couple of minutes longer."

"It's not the time, but the pressure," the Hunter pointed out. "Remember, I wasn't strong enough to pull the skewer out by myself."

"I'll go slow," Bob promised, and with that his companion had to be content.

Actually the principal difficulty with the walk was provided by Bob's joints, which were still painful. They met no one on the way. It seemed likely that everyone on the island—perhaps even the setter of the trip wire, by this time—was out on the beach celebrating. It would be the same ten days later on Bastille Day, since French blood was as strong as American on the island, and those who felt more Polynesian than anything else were perfectly willing to accept any excuse for a good time.

Unfortunately, there was no one at the Seevers' either, when they got there. Bob used the telephone, first to notify the refinery of his accident and his whereabouts, then to call a few likely places for the doctor. It seemed rather probable that he and his family might be out on the reef, where people often partied or picnicked, but the store and the library seemed worth trying. Practically none of the island's private homes had telephones.

Before he made contact with anyone who could offer a useful suggestion, the door opened and Jenny entered. Neither she nor Bob actually asked, "What are *you* doing here?" but the question was plain on both faces. Bob and the Hunter had expected her to be out at the search area, and of course she had expected Bob to be at work.

"Wind's too high, and onshore," she answered the unasked question. "After all, we've had better luck with the weather than we've had any right to expect, so far."

Bob explained his own presence by displaying his left arm. The Hunter thought this would be poor judgment, but the girl had seen such things before in her father's office and took it quite calmly. She eyed the projecting bone for a moment and then said quite steadily, "You'd better sit down or lie down. Dad will have to set that; I suppose the Hunter has done everything else."

"I think so. Where is your father? I was phoning around for him."

"Down on the beach with a bucket of burn ointment. Fireworks day. Didn't you either remember or hear?"

"I didn't remember that aspect of it, and even with the Hunter this arm takes up a lot of my attention. Can you bring him back here, or should I go to him?"

"You stay put. I'll have him right back." The girl vanished again, without wasting time asking how the injury had occurred. She was back in ten minutes with her parents and Maeta, who had been with them. It was much later, however, before the story was told.

The doctor and the Hunter had to decide whether

to use a local anesthetic, which would force the alien to withdraw from the arm, or let the Hunter block the sensory nerves from the area. The latter would be better except that he was not sure he could handle the general crepitation—the grating of the bones as they were set, which would travel through much of the skeleton and be almost impossible to prevent Bob from feeling. Seever pointed out that a local injection would do little for this phenomenon either, and that it would be better for the Hunter to be on hand to take care of bleeding and infection. Seever would do his best not to let the bones grate.

The Hunter agreed to this. Bob had to serve as communication relay as his guest helped guide Seever's manipulation. Eventually, however, he was able to tell the story while the doctor worked on a cast for his arm.

Seever was quite indignant at not having been told about the heart damage before working on the arm, but had to admit that the information would not have made him act at all differently.

Both girls thought of André immediately, and said so, but both admitted there was doubt. The trip-wire they would have credited to him without hesitation, but the stabbing was, as Bob had felt, a different matter.

"You didn't even see the wire, much less the person, did you?" asked Maeta.

"No," Bob answered. "All I actually saw was the cut tire, and the skewer after it was out of my chest. The Hunter heard footsteps while I was still out, but didn't see anything. At any rate it was no accident. Someone wanted to kill me—or, as the Hunter points out, wanted to kill someone. He may not have cared who."

"Maybe not," pointed out the older girl, "but it was your handlebars that were loosened back there at the library." Bob had never discussed this matter with the others. He answered as he had to the Hunter.

"They weren't loosened. They were turned slightly

and tightened in a different position." He filled in the other details.

"That couldn't have been an accident either," Mrs. Seever said.

"Right. If my bar had been loose, then maybe; but it wouldn't tighten in a different position on its own."

"Then someone was trying to hurt you even then."

"I can't see that. It was a silly way to try. Fifty to one I'd have been facing forward as I started and never fallen at all. Someone might have been trying to *annoy* me."

"Was André there?" asked Jenny.

"No. A bunch of kids collected to laugh, but he wasn't one of them."

"But you were inside the library, and your bike outside, for hours," Jenny pointed out. "He could have been there any time."

"So could anyone on the island except Maeta, who was writing things on file cards while I described books to her. I'm not worrying about that trick; it's something I could believe of any kid. What happened today is a different ballpark. A minor practical joke and a neck-breaking effort combined with a stabbing just don't go together."

"I'm not so sure," the doctor said slowly. "These have one thing in common."

"What?" The Hunter's voice joined the others on their way in from Bob's eardrum.

"In both cases, you faced the possibility of being injured or killed, but because of the Hunter you're essentially undamaged." Bob glanced at his arm and raised his eyebrows. "You know what I mean. The Hunter has been doing his job. Whoever pushed the skewer through you an hour or two ago is going to have a fascinating body of information to use when he sees you walking around later today. Couldn't both these tricks have been *experiments?* I can think of one person who might very well want to conduct some tests on you, Bob, now that you're back on Ell."

"Who?" asked the younger girl. The others were

silent. Seever's meaning flashed on Bob and the Hunter at the same moment, and neither was surprised at the doctor's next question.

"Hunter, just how certain are you that the one you were chasing was actually destroyed in that fire?"

10. Joke Three

"It never occurred to me to doubt it," Bob relayed from the Hunter. "I'm sure I would have died under the same conditions. We saw him on the ground. Bob poured oil on and around him, and lighted it. The soil was packed hard, and contained enough moisture to make penetration a slow job."

"You tried it yourself?"

"Not at that spot," the alien had to admit, "but—"

"But you still feel sure," Seever interrupted Bob's relay. "All right, you may be—may have been— quite right. General experience carries weight no one can reasonably ignore, though I do wish you'd tested that soil on the spot and at the time. I also think we'd better learn more about the desChenes boy who was watching. It would be best if you could check him yourself, but pretty awkward to arrange. I'll try, but if you can make any suggestions—this sounds like our talk seven years ago, doesn't it?"

Bob admitted that it did, and brought the discussion back to order.

"I admit it would be worthwhile to find just what that young clown has been up to, and whether your suspicion could have any basis," he said. "We still have the search, though. What about that? It's too rough today, you said, Jen?"

"Yes," the girl amplified, "even with a couple more paddlers we couldn't have held position long while Mae was down. It's going to be bad for another couple of days, we think."

"Hm." Bob frowned. "And we have less than half the planned area mapped. Well, I don't see what we can do—that's a pity; I should think this arm would get me off work for a week or two, and that would give us a lot of useful time. I wish those diving outfits would come."

"We'd still need a boat to get out there, unless you're thinking of swimming a mile or so from North Beach, searching until you're worn out, and then swimming back," Maeta pointed out.

"You could do it."

"No doubt, but I wouldn't. I'm sane. Not for anything short of life and death—I mean—" She fell silent, and a blush showed even on her dark skin. Bob laughed, genuinely and without bitterness.

"All right, Mae, I know this isn't like rescuing a drowning child. We all know the search is just a hope, and maybe not such a good one as I want to believe, and it would be silly for you to take too much risk. I feel bad enough about the chances you've already been taking. There are sharks there sometimes, and they're not always polite enough to show a fin as they approach. Tell me, could a power boat hold position out there with this wind and chop? If it could, we could send the Hunter down the way we did before."

"It would be all right as long as the engine held out," the girl said slowly. "I'd certainly be willing to take a minor chance like that, for something this important. We might be able to borrow the Paukés' *Vaevae*, if they're not using it now. We'd have to go out by the channel; she draws too much for the passage by North Beach. I'll ask them if we can use her tomorrow, if you like. Are you sure you won't have to work? You still have one good arm."

"How about it, Doc? What's PFI policy in this situation?"

"Pretty tolerant," replied Seever. "If it weren't for the Hunter, you'd be in bed for a week, and certainly off work."

"If it weren't for the Hunter I'd be well on my way to being stiff by now. But never mind, and pardon the interruption; I know what you mean. Go on."

"Of course I can't report all your injuries, partly because they'd be unbelievable and the Hunter has made them unprovable. The arm should be an excuse for a few days, though; I think you can count on some search time."

"If the weather doesn't get any worse," amended Jenny.

It didn't, though it got no better for several days. The Paukés were willing to lend their boat with the understanding that Maeta would be in charge of it, and for several more days the search went on.

By Wednesday the wind had dropped, and it was possible to use Maeta's outrigger again; Jenny had not yet gotten around to patching her kayak. On Thursday, Bob went back to regular working hours. On Saturday, July tenth, the girls detected a large mass of metal.

They were farther out now, and the water was deep enough to restrict Maeta's bottom activities even when she wore a weighted belt, so the operation had been slowing down. Morale, even for the quietly determined Teroa girl, had been deteriorating. Jenny would probably have failed to come out several times if the possibility of Maeta's discovering the spaceship in her absence had not occurred to her.

They had another paddle, as Mrs. Seever had been helping for most of the week, but the work was getting more exhausting for the diver all the time. The detector could not be left unchecked for more than a very few minutes at a time; the bottom was so irregular that it was likely either to get tangled in coral or be so far from the mud as to be ineffective.

Consequently, when the strong signal came and had been carefully verified, they decided to stop and buoy the area and then, though it was still early in the afternoon, bring the canoe back to North Beach and get word to Bob and the Hunter. Jenny also mentioned the chance to fix her own kayak at last.

Part way down the road, she discovered that the brake of her bicycle was not working. It was a minor inconvenience, since the road was fairly level, but it caused all of them to think.

The group broke up at the Seever home-hospital. Mrs. Seever stayed there, Jenny went to the beach where her kayak was lying, and Maeta went out the causeway to the refinery to report to Bob and the Hunter. She found them easily enough, since no fuss was made about adults' going anywhere on the island, and her presence gave the two a strong suspicion why she was there; but there were too many people around for her to report details. It was nearly two hours before Bob could leave his station and walk back to the shore with her and hear the full report. She gave it as soon as they were more or less out of hearing from the group.

"There's a place about thirty-five feet long and ten wide where the detector buzzes when it's within a foot of the bottom," she started. "That's at the edges. It sounds off two or three feet up when it's near the center of the area."

"That sounds good," the Hunter answered through Bob. "The ship I was chasing was about twenty-five of your feet long and four in diameter—much larger than my own."

"It could also be one of those midget Japanese subs from the big war," Bob pointed out. "I never heard of their operating in this area, though. Old Toke has always said that his own secrecy measures back in the thirties, arranging for wrong 'corrections' to maritime charts and that sort of thing, kept them from sending a task force here to get the oil source. I'd doubt it myself. I know the published charts don't show Ell, but I'd be very surprised if the navy of any major nation didn't know about the place. I just don't think we were a big enough target early in World War II, handy as we were for our own folks. Anyway, even if a sub is a possibility, this has to be checked out. Thanks a lot, Mae."

"There won't be time today," Maeta pointed out, nodding toward the low sun. "It'll be dark almost as soon as we could get out there."

"That's all right. I'm off tomorrow anyway," Bob said happily. "We'll let the Hunter down to feel it over and make sure, and then—well, he can tell us what sort of sign or note to make and leave down there for his people when they come back. Maybe he'll even be able to tell us when they're likely to come."

"You're very sure of that, aren't you, Bob?" the girl said softly.

"Of course. We're sure they've been here, from what happened to that generator shield you found."

"Couldn't the other one—the one the Hunter was chasing years ago—have done that?"

"You mean if the doc's right and he wasn't killed after all? I suppose so, but why should he?"

"Why should anyone else? The doctor asked that, and I don't think you gave him much of an answer. I agree with him that it's a very weak spot in your whole picture."

"Well, I agree with the Hunter. He knows his own people best, and who am I to argue with him? I feel like celebrating."

"You mean you *will* feel like celebrating if what we've found actually turns out to be one of the ships."

"Yes, of course. Right now, though, I just feel certain that it will be—it must be—and it's a darned good feeling."

"I can believe it must be. I just hope I never hear you say, in a belittling sort of tone, that wishful thinking is a feminine trait. I wish I could feel as sure as you seem to."

"The Hunter calls it a human trait. Why not be human, Mae?"

In spite of the slightly pejorative remark which had just been attributed to him, the Hunter was sharing his host's feeling at the moment. He, too, felt unreasonably sure that the object the girls had found would turn out to be one of the ships. He knew that there was an excellent chance that it was something else shed by Earth's metal-wasting culture, but fully expected to be feeling around inside a more or less damaged faster-than-light flyer in another thirteen or fourteen hours.

As they reached the shore end of the causeway, Bob looked off to his right along the beach. Jenny's kayak was lying bottom up where it had been for several days, two or three hundred yards from where he and Maeta stood, but the owner was nowhere in sight. Many other craft were on the lagoon, though most were heading for shore, dock, or anchorage as the sun sank.

"Maybe she's finished already," Maeta answered the unuttered question. "She's had a couple of hours, and it was just a matter of cementing a patch."

"Likely enough," Bob admitted. Maeta had not mentioned Jenny's brake trouble, and it had not occurred to her that anything else was likely to happen to the younger girl. Bob, so far, had seemed to be the principal target, if anyone was really shooting. Maeta, therefore, had forgotten about the brake, and failed to mention it as they walked. The three of them had another few hundred yards of calm as they strolled toward the Seever home.

It evaporated at the door, where Jenny's mother met them.

"I thought you weren't coming at all!" she exclaimed. "I suppose you just got away from your work, Bob. Look, you're both to go to Jenny's boat, Ben says, and look very carefully for something sharp. We want to find out what it was."

Bob and Maeta started to ask the obvious question together, but the woman held up her hand to stop them. "I'm sorry, I know that's out of order. I'm upset. Just as Jenny got to her boat an hour or so ago—she stopped here for a while first—she stepped on something in the sand that cut her right foot, just behind the base of the big toe, all the way to the bone. Her father is still sewing tendons together. A couple of young people brought her home, but she's lost a lot of blood and hasn't been able to tell us much. Ben and I want to know what she stepped on. So do you. It isn't as though this was the States, paved with broken bottles; this is a civilized community."

"Will she be all right?" asked Bob, and "Did she lose too much blood?" was Maeta's more specific inquiry.

"Yes to you, Bob, and I don't think so, Mae. You two get down there and find out what she stepped on, please."

Neither of them argued. They headed straight toward the beach, short-cutting the road but of course avoiding gardens. There were large spots of blood along the faint path which they followed; Jenny had evidently been helped home this way.

The beach was well peopled, though the sun was almost down. Most of the boats were now ashore or at anchor. No one, however, seemed aware of Jenny's accident; at least there was no crowd around her canoe, and no excited clusters of people. It was a perfectly ordinary Ell Saturday just before suppertime.

Bob and Maeta were adequately shod, so they did not hesitate to approach the kayak. The sand a yard or so from its near side was blood-caked, and this seemed a reasonable place to start looking. With a brief, "On the job, Hunter, and skip the speeches," Bob knelt beside the brown patch and began scooping sand away from it. The Hunter had to admit that his host was working with reasonable caution, considering the circumstances, so he said nothing and got on the job —ready to take care of things if Bob found the thing they wanted the hard way.

After a minute or two, with the immediate site of the stain excavated to a depth of six or eight inches, Maeta began to dig as well. After disposing of Bob's objections, which sounded very much like those the Hunter used on Bob himself when he felt his host was being careless, she started along the side of the boat and searched for a couple of feet in either direction from the spot on the boat which had obviously been prepared to take a patch. Then she began working out toward Bob. Unfortunately they had not come very close to meeting when the sun set.

"We'll have to try again in the morning," Bob said, straightening up with an effort. "I wonder when we can get out to check the ship-or-whatever you found?"

"Stay here," was Maeta's injunction. "I'll go home and get a light. Our place is closer than the doctor's."

"You think it's worth the trouble? No one else is likely to get hurt before morning."

"Yes, it is," the girl said firmly. The Hunter, a little surprised at Bob's obtuseness, added, "Of course it is, Bob. Remember your bike trip-wire. We must either find what she stepped on, or make certain that it's gone." Maeta had disappeared by the time this sentence was completed, but Bob answered aloud anyway.

"Oh, of course. I hadn't thought of that. I guess I was expecting to be the only victim, if there was anything to that idea. If this really wasn't an accident— I suppose that's what Jenny's mother was talking about—where do you suppose they'd hide it?"

"Close to the boat, where anyone working on the patch would be most likely to step on it," the Hunter answered rather impatiently.

"Oh—then that's why Mae started digging where she did."

"I would assume so." The alien restrained himself with a slight effort; after all, his host was not completely as he should be, and in any case had freely admitted that he was not always quick on the uptake.

They tried to continue the search while waiting for Maeta, but even with Venus helping the gibbous moon, progress was slow. Fortunately the girl was back in a few minutes with a flashlight, and to Bob's relief was willing to hold it while he did the digging. He worked very carefully, with the girl's and the Hunter's vision supplementing his own, and after another hour all three were prepared to certify that there was nothing within a fifteen-foot radius of the point under the patch site which could possibly penetrate the human skin, except for a few shells. None of these showed a trace of blood, even to the Hunter.

This was more than interesting, since skin had certainly been penetrated.

"He'd have been smarter to leave it here. It could have been an accident, then," Bob remarked.

"Like tightening up your bike again," Maeta pointed out. "Is this really someone who's not very bright, which I could believe of André, or is there some reason we haven't thought of for making it obvious these aren't accidents?"

Bob had not thought of that possibility, and had no answer to the suggestion. They returned thoughtfully to the Seevers' with their report.

The doctor had finished his work, and Jenny was on a couch with the damaged foot heavily bandaged and splinted to immobilize toes and ankle. During the ensuing discussion, in which the Hunter took little part, Bob and he heard for the first time of her bicycle trouble. Everyone admitted that coincidence was being stretched far beyond its yield point. Bob was the most reluctant, in spite of the evidence, to believe that there was deliberate interference with the project to save his life, but even he was halfhearted in asking Seever whether other people on the island had been showing a larger than normal incidence of burns, falls, cuts, and other accidents. The answer was a qualified negative; as Seever put it, nothing of the sort had caught his attention.

"Of course, with a population this small—" Bob was starting, when Jenny made one of her few interruptions of the evening.

"Swallow that with your degree, Bob. You know as well as I do that these aren't accidents. They're just the sort of thing young André has been doing for years, to his family and to me and sometimes to other people. It's just that they're worse now, and you've been added to the list. I admit I don't really know he's the one, but I feel pretty sure, and tomorrow I'm going to know."

"You're not going anywhere tomorrow," her father said firmly.

"All right, then he'll come here. You tell his father he's due for a shot, or something. I've put up with a lot from that kid even if this isn't part of it, and I'm going to find out why."

"You've changed your mind about Shorty?" Bob asked.

"Not entirely, but he wouldn't do things like that to you, I don't think. You get André here, Dad, and then leave him with me. We've been through this before, and I thought we'd settled it a year ago. I suppose Bob and Mae will be out beyond the reef tomorrow, and you certainly won't let me go, but I'm going to get something done."

"Even if it has no connection with the main job," Bob remarked.

"Even then, if it really hasn't. What else could have gotten him interested in you?"

"I still don't see why you're so sure he's the one," Maeta said.

"I expect an art student would call it recognition of style," the redhead answered. "Never mind. You just get that ship checked out, and let me know the answer as soon as you can."

"How sure of *that* are you?" asked Bob.

"Not sure enough. We'll report to each other. Dad, I'm sleepy and this foot hurts. Anything you can do?"

Bob and Maeta took the hint. At the road outside

they paused for a moment, their homes lying in opposite directions.

"D'you think Jenny could be right about the desChenes kid?" Bob asked. "How well do you know him?"

"Pretty well. After all, you're almost the only one on the island these days who doesn't know practically everybody. He certainly is a pest; Jenny and Shorty are both right about that. He does seem to get fun out of being a nuisance, and even out of hurting people. I've never had much trouble from him myself, unless it was he who hid my paddles a couple of times. He damaged some library books about three years ago, soon after I started working there, and I took away his card for a couple of months. The first paddle incident came right after that. I found them easily enough both times, and never bothered to find out who did it."

"I would have!"

"And thereby made the day for the one who'd done it," Maeta retorted. The Hunter agreed with her, but kept the thought to himself.

"Where does he live?" asked Bob. "I know what he looks like—a little bit plump for his height."

"East of the dock road, close to the beach. Yes, he's a little on the heavy side. He's not very active; I see him in the library a lot of the time. He doesn't seem to get around with his own age group much."

"Doesn't he like them, or don't they like him?"

"I've never thought about that. I'd guess it's his own choosing. As I said, he's reading a lot of the time—at least, he usually has several books at once out of the library, and pretty often is curled up somewhere inside the place with a book. Jenny may be right, but I'm not at all sure. Her father, remember, is blaming someone else for what happened to you and her; he thinks you didn't manage to kill that other creature the Hunter was after. I sort of agree with him. Would your masculine pride be offended if I walked home with you now?"

Bob felt uncomfortable at the suggestion, and might have dismissed it too tersely for real politeness, but the Hunter expressed himself sharply.

"Bob, even if you don't want to believe she could protect you from anything, she would at least be a witness. Her presence could prevent something from happening, or give us a better chance of finding how it happened. Never mind what she calls your masculine pride; use your human brains."

"All right, Mae." Bob spoke aloud. "The Hunter is on your side. I was just going to suggest I take *you* home, since the accidents seem to be spreading, but I suppose there's no evidence they're interested in you. All right, let's go."

The walk was uneventful. There was very little talk; all three were listening carefully for evidence of others on or near the road. The moon, though high in the northeast, was of little help; this was the jungle branch of the island, and the trees shadowed the road itself as well as the underbrush on each side. Once past the school there were no streetlights.

Bob pointed out to Maeta the scene of the bicycle trap, though there was nothing useful to see in the shadows and even her flashlight revealed little. He and the Hunter had checked the scene over very carefully, in full daylight, the day after the incident, but even the experienced detective had found nothing informative or even suggestive. It bothered his pride.

Maeta left them at the Kinnaird's door, refusing the suggestion that she come in. Her last remark was the recommendation that Bob's father come with them the next day if he were free. As usual, Bob had to hold this item until his sister was upstairs for the night. It then led to some discussion, and was modified firmly by the lady of the house.

"Arthur has been having all the fun," she pointed out. "I love our daughter, but I think it's my turn to get a day on the water with you young folks, and let your father entertain Daphne tomorrow. All right, Dear?"

The Hunter suspected that it was not entirely all right. As far as he knew, Arthur Kinnaird had not had any "fun" on the project either. However, no one was greatly surprised when the man made no objection to his wife's idea.

He took the child off after breakfast, and the rest of the group headed northwest along the road as soon as father and daughter were out of sight. Bob's bicycle had not yet been repaired, but he used his father's and they reached North Beach in a few minutes. Maeta was waiting for them, and after a quick but careful inspection of the canoe itself and the search equipment, they shoved off.

The women paddled, while Bob undid the wires fastening the pipe to the rest of the gear. The plug and telegraph had been repaired, but he tested the latter again. Then he tied the new rope, which had been supporting the concrete box, very securely around the pipe, and placed one hand in the open end of the latter.

The Hunter left through the skin of the hand, the process as usual taking several minutes, and signaled with the buzzer when it was complete. Bob told the others. The alien could hear their voices, but did not yet bother to make an eye.

"We're ready here," Bob said. "Are we close to your marker, Mae?"

"Pretty near. We have to hide Tank Four behind Seven, and line the north corner of Eleven against the middle of Nine. It will be a few minutes yet."

She had provided these bearings the night before, and the Hunter had mapped them. He knew without looking, therefore, that they were about a mile north and a little west of North Beach, a little less than that straight-west of Apu, and about half a mile from the nearest breakers.

Eventually the young woman called, "There it is. Be ready, Bob." The Hunter felt his pipe being lifted. Then came, "All right, we're right over it," and almost instantly warm water closed over him and his protection.

He made an eye, but there was little to see until he reached the bottom. The pipe was nearly horizontal, and turning slowly; sometimes he could see the line from the buoy marking the location, sometimes his eye was directed away from it. The boat was not visible, as the Hunter had formed the eye a little way inside the pipe to minimize stray light, and the open end of the pipe itself was slanted slightly downward.

Bob had felt the tension go off the line when the Hunter reached bottom, and had stopped paying out. However, the alien found himself almost buried in the soft mud, and buzzed the signal to pull up slightly. The spin had stopped, of course, but slowly resumed as torsion in the rope tried to relieve itself, and he slowly scanned the whole circumference.

The light was more than adequate, and he could see a long, low hillock on the mud, corresponding roughly in size to Maeta's description. There was less coral this far from the reef, but some had grown on and over the ridge; the feature must have been there for some years at least.

He was ten or twelve feet to one side of the nearest part of the elevation. He extended his eye briefly, to see which way the canoe was pointing, buzzed directions, and in a minute or less was over the ridge near its center. Then he gave the "down" signal, and in a moment was on the bottom once more, not so deeply buried this time.

Feeling at least as much tension as any of the others had been showing, he extended a pseudopod into the limy mud. It was at least six inches thick even at the top of the hillock, but under that six-inch layer was metal. He was tempted to leave the pipe entirely, but very luckily did not. He kept groping with hair-fine tendrils, adding detail to the picture he was developing. Yes, the girls were right. It was his quarry's ship, the upper portion at least nearly intact. He could feel and read symbols identifying service connections, and presently found one of the small valves which his own species used for entrance and exit. The larger ports, for cargo and for the trained animals they sometimes used to manipulate controls, would be in the lower part of the hull, which seemed to be right-side up.

The access valve was shut. He felt around for the power control and activated it, but was not very surprised when nothing happened. It was much harder to operate the manual control, but after several minutes he had the opening cracked enough to let himself flow in. He thought once again of leaving the pipe entirely and entering the ship with his whole substance, but once again decided to wait. It was not real foresight, at least not conscious foresight, but it was lucky.

He buzzed a "yes" to those above, blaming himself for not ending their suspense sooner, and reached farther into the hull through the partly open valve.

He had time to realize what was happening to him, but not enough to do anything about it.

11. First Aid

The three in the outrigger received and correctly interpreted the Hunter's last signal, and for some time were far too excited and exultant to pay any attention to events on the bottom. None of them was ever sure just how much time passed before anyone began to wonder why no more signals were coming through; and even for Bob it took still longer for curiosity to become anxiety.

Eventually he gave a few jerks to the rope—the surface-to-depth telegraph was still only a plan. Naturally, there was no response. He decided that his symbiont must have left the pipe and was exploring the ship in detail. No plans had been made for signaling or any other action in such a situation, and Bob spent some time abusing himself verbally for the omission. The Hunter agreed later that they had both been pretty stupid, but insisted on taking his share of the blame, since he had after all been in a much better position to foresee what actually happened. After all, Seever had mentioned "normal police procedures."

Something like half an hour was spent waiting and occasionally pulling on the rope before the three became really disturbed. Maeta finally went overboard and swam down to see, if possible, what was going on, but even diving goggles did not let her examine the pipe in real detail. She was quite sure, when she pulled it out of the mud, that the Hunter was inside, and to make really certain she checked by touch.

For two reasons she failed to detect the tendrils the Hunter had extended from his main mass: they had broken when she lifted the pipe; and they were too fine anyway. The damage to the Hunter when they broke was negligible; the memory patterns which formed his identity were stored with multiple redundancy throughout his tissue. Cutting him into two equal parts would have been bad unless they could have rejoined almost at once, but the few milligrams he had lost in the ship would not have bothered him even if he had been conscious.

The ship had been booby-trapped with a half-living substance designed to immobilize members of his species; but it had no effect on the far coarser human cells, so Maeta herself was able to return to the surface, get her breath, and report.

Bob, wasting no more time, hauled up the pipe. He had been hoping that the trouble was merely electrical failure up to this point; but when he left his hand in contact with the jelly for several minutes without becoming aware of the Hunter's presence by any sort of word or signal, he knew that something much more serious was wrong. They headed for shore at once, with Bob wondering aloud why the Hunter had never given him a course in first aid for symbionts.

They headed at top speed for the Seevers' home, giving no thought to practical jokers. Fortunately their bicycles seemed intact. Maeta carried the pipe, since Bob had only one really usable arm and none of the bicycle carriers was adequate. The girl found it quite awkward; she had to carry the pipe open end up, after discovering that the Hunter's unconscious form—to use the noun loosely—was slowly pouring out when she held it horizontally.

None of them really expected that Seever could be of much help, but no other line of action occurred to them.

They were rather disconcerted, upon entering the reception room, to find Jenny seated beside her usual desk with the damaged foot on a hassock in front of her. She was talking, apparently quite amiably, to André desChenes, who did not react at all at the sight of the newcomers. No one else was in the room.

Jenny saw the pipe, but did not realize at first that it was occupied. Her first assumption, she admitted later, was that something had gone wrong with the detector. Then she realized that they would hardly have brought such a problem to her father, and decided that something more serious had happened; but the delay kept her from asking reflexively any hasty and injudicious questions with the boy present. She came, she confessed, within a split second of asking whether the ship they had found was an instrument error.

"Is anyone with your father?" Maeta asked before any of them could make a slip.

"No. He's in the next room, or if he isn't, call," replied Jenny.

The three went on into the inner room, and met

Seever just entering by the other door. He looked at Maeta's burden and frowned.

"Trouble?" Bob described the situation tersely, and Seever looked closely into the pipe at its unresponsive occupant.

"You've touched him and nothing happened."

"I kept my hand on him all the way to shore and nothing happened."

"Hmph." The doctor was out of his depth as far as direct experience went, but he was a logical man. "I can't tell offhand whether he's unconscious, paralyzed, or dead. We'll assume one of the first two, since the last doesn't give us anything to go on. Assuming he's alive, the first thing is to keep him that way. We know he needs oxygen. He may be getting enough through that six or eight square inches, since he can't be using much at the moment, but I'd say we'd better pour him into something which will give him more exposed surface. What's his volume—a couple of quarts? A pie plate won't be enough, and I don't suppose separating him among several would be a very good idea. He must have *some* essential continuity to his structure, even if shape doesn't mean anything to him. Here, maybe this will do." He had found a large enamel basin, and they inverted the pipe over it. After a few moments Bob suggested that the plug at the upper end also be removed. Seever finally managed this while Maeta held up the pipe itself.

The alien tissue was very viscous and flowed slowly. Seever thought this might be a good sign, implying that whatever forces permitted the being to control his shape must still be operating. He was right, as it happened, but none of them could be sure. Bob's mention of rigor mortis helped no one's morale.

Eventually the mass of green semifluid was in the basin, spreading slowly toward the edges.

"Bob, you're the chemist," said Seever. "What else

has he told you about his needs? I assume they include water."

"Not the way we do. It's not inside his cells; they're not really cells in the way ours are, just complex single molecules. There is water, but it's bonded to the surface for the most part and doesn't form part of the inside architecture."

"Then there's no osmotic problem—it won't matter if we give him fresh water or salt?"

"No. He can exist in both, as well as in our body fluids. You probably needn't give him any, but I suppose it won't do any damage and might be safer. I'd be more worried, though, about food."

"Why?" asked Seever.

"That's really his smallest reserve. He can last for a while outside a host body without—well, fuel—but the time is limited. He has nothing corresponding to human fat or glycogen as a reserve. When he was under water in the pipe he was always catching and eating small organisms which were trying to eat him, he said."

"I see. I suppose any of his so-called cells can carry out digestion, as they seem to do everything else. Well, then, all we can do is sprinkle a little water on him, drop in a piece of cheese—protein seems most likely to have everything he'd need chemically—and hope. It's logical, but somehow it doesn't seem like medical practice."

Whatever it seemed like to Seever, it was what they did. They used only a small amount of water, so as not to shut the patient off too completely from air. This was unfortunate, since more water would have absorbed the paralyzing agent more quickly. Its distribution coefficient between water and the tissue of the Hunter's species was very small—it had to be, to be as quick a trap as it was—but it was far from zero.

That left the group with nothing to do but sit and theorize. Most were concerned about the Hunter himself. Bob's mother had already started to wonder what the alien's prolonged separation would do to her son, but did not at first mention this to the others.

Maeta suggested that they go back to the waiting room to see what Jenny had learned from André, but the older people thought this injudicious, since André might still be there, and Bob did not want to leave his symbiont. His mother offered to stay with the patient while Bob got something to eat, but while they were still discussing the matter the door opened and Jenny crutched herself in.

Her question about what had happened at the reef collided with several about her progress with her young suspect, but Jenny won, and some minutes were spent by Maeta and Bob, telling the story of the morning's events. Jenny took her first really good look at the Hunter with great interest, and was with some difficulty persuaded to take her attention from the hospital basin and report on her interview. Her words were suggestive but inconclusive.

"I can't really prove anything," she admitted, "but I'm more certain than before that he's done most of these things. He's harder to get hold of than a jellyfish. He never actually denied any of the tricks, but he wouldn't admit them in so many words, either."

"Which ones did you ask him about?" asked Bob. "The boat? The rope? My handlebars? Your foot?"

"Not all of them. I started with my foot, since I had the sample available, and pointed out how I could have bled to death if there hadn't been anyone around to help. He agreed that this was bad, and remarked that if people were going to leave glass around the island everyone would have to start wearing shoes the way they do in Europe and the States. I didn't ask why he thought it was glass instead of metal or a shell; I wanted to save his slips, if that was one, to dump on him all at once later.

"I mentioned your broken arm, and he said you must have gotten out of bike practice while you were away. How many people did you tell how that happened, Bob?"

"I didn't tell anyone the whole story, except of course you folks here, and Dad. I told the fellows at work that I'd had a fall."

"Did you mention it was off a bike?" she asked emphatically. Bob thought silently for a moment.

"I don't think so. I wouldn't have wanted to sound as though I couldn't ride, and I certainly didn't want to tell anyone about the wire, especially when we couldn't find it."

"Well, André knows or is taking for granted that you were on your bike when it happened. I didn't ask how he knew. When I talked about the rope and the leak in my boat, he just asked what we were doing out there all those days, and were we looking for something special, and when was I going to keep my promise that he could come out with us. When you came in with the pipe a while ago, he asked whether that was what we were looking for. I said it wasn't, and then realized I'd admitted we were looking for something. I told you he was slippery."

"How about my handlebars and your brake? Is he a bike expert?"

"I didn't get around to either of them. I'm still sure, from those slips he made, that he's at the bottom of all this, though."

"Maybe he found out about my being on the bike from Silly. She knows, and goodness knows how many of her small friends she may have told," Bob remarked.

"And I still doubt that he's actually at the *bottom*, in any case," added the doctor. "I agree he's probably involved, though. I wish I could figure out what happened to the Hunter today; I don't see how the kid could possibly be involved in that. There weren't any boats besides your own out there, were there?"

Bob and his mother said there weren't; Maeta qualified the statement slightly.

"None *stayed* there. Two or three times fishermen or other people who had come out the main channel tacked down and called hello, and asked what we were doing, but they always went right on."

"What did you tell them?"

"Just that we were collecting. That could have covered anything—Pauhéré's curios, or the Museum Exchange, or just amusing ourselves."

"Do you remember who they were?" asked Seever.

"Most of them, I think. Is it important?"

"I wish I could guess. I wonder if anyone on Ell could have free-diving equipment that the whole world doesn't know about."

"If they have," Maeta assured him, "it's a pretty close secret. As you say, usually everyone knows something like that. I see what you're driving at now, but I don't see any way to be really sure—except that I'd swear no boat stayed close enough for long enough to let a diver get over near us and get back again if he was swimming. Maybe if someone's invented a personal outboard motor for divers it could have been done, but they'd have been taking a chance that I'd be down at any moment and see them."

"Maybe it wouldn't be they taking the chance," Seever pointed out grimly. "Well, we're speculating again. Make a list of the people you saw go by, first chance you get, and let me have it. When you don't know what you're doing, record data, I always say. I know the more pieces there are, the tougher the puzzle; but if the pieces belong, you have to have them. Any other plans, Bob?"

"I don't see what we can do about the Hunter except wait," was the answer. "If you should think of anything better, Doc, go ahead without waiting for my opinion."

"I don't agree with that," said Maeta. "Bob has lived with the Hunter for years, and must know more about him than anyone—even Bob himself—realizes. Some idea of the doctor's might recall something to him that he hasn't thought of yet—or might remind him of something which would warn us that the idea was bad, or dangerous to the Hunter."

"A good point," agreed Seever. "But how about the rest of the job? You're interpreting that 'yes' on the buzzer as meaning the ship was really there. Does that give us any line of action, even without the Hunter?"

Neither Bob nor Jenny had any ideas at first, but Maeta produced one almost instantly.

"As I understand it," she said, "the plan was for the Hunter to leave a message at this ship, on the assumption that his people are on the earth and would check there at times. Hadn't we better put a note there ourselves? We don't know whether he had a chance to before he was knocked out."

"We don't know the language," pointed out Jenny.

"Why should we need to? If they're really investigating this world, there's a good chance they'll have learned French or English."

"That's a thought," Bob agreed. "We could write out the whole story and put it in a weighted bottle, right on top of the ship. They couldn't help noticing it."

"It may not be *quite* that easy," Maeta pointed out. "The ship is buried under the mud, and the bottle might not be obvious. They might not pay attention to anything *not* buried like the ship. The Hunter could probably have put his message inside the ship, but we might not even be able to put it exactly on top. Remember, the Hunter had us move around a little before he finally signaled he'd found it—if that was what his signal meant."

"What else could he have meant?" asked Bob indignantly. "And can't we remember which way he moved us?"

"Nothing else, I hope; that's all that makes sense to me, too. A one-word message can usually be misinterpreted, though. Yes, we can find the spot again. I just don't want you to think all the troubles are over."

"No fear of that," Bob assured her. "I never have the chance to get that idea."

"Sorry. Still hurting?"

"Yes. Muscles, joints, arm, and face, though the last is pretty well back together. Well, I'll try to get my mind off it by writing a message to the Hunter's crowd. The sooner we get it out there, the better. If they do visit the ship it must be at night, and with the luck I have these days it'll be tonight if we don't get out there this afternoon. I wonder how often they do check back? Or if anything the Hunter did today could have set off a signal to bring them back?"

"That's a thought," agreed Seever. "Much better than your last one. Why would they have to come by night? They could make their approach under water at any time—or can their spaceships only move straight up and down, or something like that?" Bob looked startled.

"I never thought of that, and I don't really know about the ships. Well, we should get the message out there anyway. Somebody find a bottle."

The note was written as briefly as possible, in pencil, on a single sheet of paper. The doctor then waxed the paper. A bottle had been found, the amount of sand needed to sink it ascertained, and paper and sand inserted. A tiny hole was drilled in the cork of the bottle to facilitate the entry of one of the Hunter's people, and the cork was tightly inserted; then the bottle was shaken around, top downward, until the paper had worked its way above the sand, presumably out of reach of water which would be forced part way into the bottle by the pressure at the bottom.

"That seems to do it," Jenny said happily when all this was accomplished. "I wish I could go with you."

"But of course you're too intelligent to suggest it seriously," her father added. Jenny made no answer.

"Sorry, Jen," Bob put in, "but there really isn't much to this anyway. By the time there's anything more to do, if there ever is, you should be all right again. There's just one more thing we need, then we can take off."

"What's that?" asked Seever.

"A good, heavy rock."

"What for? The bottle will sink."

"I know the bottle will. The trouble is, I won't. We're not just dropping the bottle over the side; we're putting it right on the ship. I'm not a good enough swimmer to reach the bottom at four fathoms, at least with one bad arm, and if I got there I wouldn't have air enough to go looking for just the right spot. I'll sink myself with the rock, and save effort and air."

"And the doctor was talking about Jenny's intelligence!" exclaimed Maeta. "He'll have to hunt for some different words for yours. I'll go down, you idiot. Why this urge to go swimming with a broken arm? If you just want to see the ship, don't bother; you can't. It's all under mud."

"I know you can do it," admitted Bob. "You can do it better than I could even with two good arms and all my health. But there's something down there that injured the Hunter, and I have no business asking anyone else to face that. You've already been taking enough chances under water for me, Mae. This is my job and the Hunter's. He's taken a chance and apparently lost; now it's my turn."

His mother started to say something, but changed her mind.

"That's right, Mom. Of course you don't want me to go down, but you're honest enough to know I'm the one who should."

Maeta was on her feet. She was not really qualified to tower over anyone, but Bob was seated and had to look up.

"Skip the heroics, Robert Kinnaird!" she snapped. "The person who should go is the person who can do it best, and don't make it sound like a Roger Young mission. I'll be down and up again, with the bottle exactly where it should be, in ninety seconds—and that's allowing for mistakes in spotting the canoe. If anyone sees a shark, I'll wait; I'm not being heroic. I was down there before, *after* the Hunter was knocked out, remember, and nothing happened to me. And how many rocks do you plan to take out there in my canoe? You'll miss the site the first time and have to come up, and you'll need another rock to go down again, and another and probably another."

"Don't rub it in."

The battle of wills was fun to watch. Told about it later, the Hunter regretted having missed it, though, as he admitted, the end was never in doubt. Fond as he was of Bob, he knew by now that he was not always a completely reasonable being. He had not known Maeta nearly as long—casual acquaintance as one of Charles Teroa's sisters seven years before hardly counted—but he already knew that she was more intelligent than his host and quicker-witted. She also possessed a more forceful personality.

Besides all this, in the present situation she was right, and both of them knew it. Bob's mother and the doctor kept out of it after the first few words, and between them managed to keep Jenny quiet too. The redhead, for reasons of her own, was on Maeta's side, but the older girl needed no help.

No rocks were carried.

Seever suddenly decided that he owed himself a pleasant ride on the water, and went along. Bob objected to this, saying that the Hunter should be kept under a medical eye, but the doctor insisted that there was nothing more he could do for the alien. In fact, he was much more worried about Bob, who now was deprived of his alien partner, lacked infection resistance of his own, and was otherwise not at his best. He refrained from mentioning this reason to either Mrs. Kinnaird or her son, and decided not to remind them of the situation by taking his bag along. He regretted this omission later.

It was midafternoon when they reached the outrigger on North Beach and embarked. The swell had increased since morning, and everyone was wet by the time they were afloat. The mile to the site was covered quickly, with all but Bob at the paddles, and the final search for the buoy took a little longer than Maeta had predicted. She worked the craft into what she recalled was the right position with respect to the marker, told Seever and Mrs. Kinnaird to hold it there, and without further ceremony slid overboard with the bottle. For a moment she trod water between the canoe's hull and the outrigger as she took in air; then she upended and drove downward.

Seever and Mrs. Kinnaird watched her as well as they could without interfering with their paddling. Bob did not. He was barely aware that she had gone at all; he was becoming less and less conscious of anything except pain. His limbs were sorer than ever, and his head felt hot. He knew the Hunter had been away from him for longer periods than this, but he felt far worse than the last time; and he was beginning to wonder whether the juggling act with his hormones was closing. He didn't know. He was beginning not to care. The sun hurt his eyes, even in the shadow of his hat brim, and he closed them.

Maeta surfaced, well within the ninety seconds she had allowed, and slid into the canoe as smoothly as she had left it. "No trouble," she said, after getting her breath. "You can see the outline of the ship under the mud, if you know what to look for. I felt into the stuff. It's very soft, and there are only a few inches of it over the top part of the ship. I felt the hard stuff, but couldn't tell by touch if it was metal or something else."

"You left the message." Bob's mother did not put it as a question.

"Sure. Neck of the bottle down against the hull, the bottom part with the paper sticking above the mud. If they look at all, or feel at all carefully, they can't miss it."

"You shouldn't have taken the chance of touching the ship," the older woman said. "Bob was right about that. You might have gotten an electric shock, or something of that sort, as the Hunter seems to have done. Could that be what happened to him, Ben?"

The doctor shrugged. "No way to tell, until he comes to and tells us. I don't know what electricity would do to him; I couldn't guess even if his tissues were like ours. There's no simple way to tell; a man can stand a shock that will kill a horse. Did he ever tell you anything about that, Bob?"

An incoherent mumble was his only answer. Mrs. Kinnaird gave a gasp of terror, but managed to retain her grip on her paddle.

Seconds later Bob was stretched out on the bottom of the dugout while Seever checked over him as well as the cramped situation allowed. He could find only the deep flush on the face and a racing pulse, which might have meant several things. The women were already paddling back toward North Beach as hard as they could. After doing what little he could for Bob, the doctor picked up the remaining paddle and used it.

At the beach, he issued orders quickly.

"We can't hand-carry him all the way to the hospital. Annette, get to your house and see if Arthur is there. If he is, have him get a car—he can usually find one. Maeta, bike down to the village and try to find either him or a car, too. Check around the desalting stations first, then go out to the refinery. Never mind explanations, just say I need a car, capital NOW. As you pass my place, tell Ev to get my kit here as fast as she can. I should have known better than to come without it."

With the women gone, Seever turned back to his patient. They had carried him into the shade, and it was now obvious even without a thermometer that he had a high fever. His face was flushed, and he was perspiring heavily. Seever was somewhat relieved by the latter fact, but he removed his own shirt and Bob's, soaked them in the sea, and spread one over the younger man's chest. He improvised a turban with the other.

It was almost sunset when a jeep appeared at high speed. Arthur Kinnaird was at the wheel, his daughter beside him, and Maeta in the back seat. They stopped a few yards short of where Bob was lying; Kinnaird was not the sort to take chances on being stuck in the sand at such a time.

"Your wife wasn't home. I've told him everything," Maeta said before Seever could ask a question.

"All right. Arthur, get us to my place as quickly as you can. I'll use the back seat, with Bob. Daph, crowd in front with Mae until we get to your house; you can get off there."

"No! I'm staying with you. Bob's sick!"

Seever was too busy even to shrug, much less argue. Maeta had shifted to the front seat and taken the child on her lap, and seconds later they were speeding back down the road. Bob's father said nothing as they approached his house, and did not slow down; the child was still with them as they approached the hospital. She tried to help carry Bob into the building; then Maeta took her out. Arthur Kinnaird remained as Seever went to work.

The trouble was plain enough now. Bob's temperature was indeed high, and the broken left arm was showing the red streaks which indicated massive infection. Seever removed the cast to reveal a red and black mess underneath.

"Antibiotics?" asked Kinnaird.

"Maybe. They don't work on everything, in spite of people's calling them 'miracle drugs'—they were doing that with the sulfa compounds a few years ago, too. I'll do the best I can, but he may not be able to keep the arm."

"This is a fine time for the Hunter to be out of action."

"Probably not coincidence," pointed out Seever. "If he were there, this wouldn't have happened at all. Look, I'll give the boy a shot of what seems best—I'll make some tests first—and then, if I can, I'll wait six hours before doing anything else. Of course, if things get obviously worse I won't be able to give all that time. Then we'll have to decide about the arm.

"And I'm going to do one more thing."

Kinnaird nodded in understanding as the doctor

put a smaller table beside the one on which Bob was
lying, placed the basin containing the Hunter on it,
and put Bob's right hand in the basin. They watched
as the hand sank slowly into the jelly. Then Seever got
out his microscope, and took scrapings from the tissue
of the other arm.

12. Joker

That was the situation when the Hunter woke up. It
took him a little while to catch up with reality,
though he knew well enough what had happened at
the ship. It had obviously been found by the search
expedition, identified as being the one stolen by the
Hunter's quarry, and booby-trapped against the possible return of that individual. The alien recalled
Seever's question about standard police procedures,
and would have blushed had he been equipped for it.
He was perfectly familiar with the immobilizing agent
which had been used, and if he had been properly
alert would never have been trapped by it.

He became aware of the basin which held him, and
of his host's hand immersed in his substance. That was
presumably what had allowed him to wake up. The
agent itself would have held him for months; but he
had absorbed an equilibrium amount of it while separate from his host's body; and his own four pounds
of tissue would have been saturated by a very small
total quantity of the substance. Since it was designed
to be absorbed rapidly by tissues similar to those of
the Hunter's usual host species, which were biochemically fairly similar to those of humanity, and since
Bob massed thirty-five or forty times as much as his

symbiont, enough had now diffused into Bob's body to clear the Hunter's nearly completely. Returning to Bob seemed safe enough, since the concentration of the substance would be so much smaller.

Without bothering to check on his surroundings by forming an eye, the Hunter began to soak his way into the hand and spread through his host's body in normal fashion. He had completed about a quarter of the job when he heard Arthur Kinnaird's voice.

"Ben! Look! The level is going down in the Hunter's dish, and he's higher around Bob's wrist than before! He must be awake!"

The alien extended a finger-sized pseudopod from the basin and waved it to let the speaker know he had been heard. The doctor's voice promptly responded.

"Hunter, get in there and get to work! Bob has picked up a very bad infection that my drugs don't seem to be touching, and he needs you. We'll ask you what happened later; first things first."

The Hunter waved again in acknowledgment. He was already aware of the trouble, and was working on it.

It was real work. Destroying the infecting organisms was a minor task, finished in minutes; but the toxins they had produced were far more difficult to neutralize, and much of the tissue in the arm where they had entered was totally destroyed. The fracture had not been responsible; neither the Hunter nor Seever had made any professional errors there. A tiny wooden splinter had gotten into Bob's left hand just beyond the end of the cast. It had clearly entered after the Hunter's departure; Bob himself might not have noticed it, but the alien could not possibly have failed to. With his personal resistance to infection long since destroyed and his symbiont absent, Bob was a walking culture tube; a few hours had nearly destroyed his arm. The Hunter had not realized that his host's general self-repair ability had become so poor, but the facts seemed beyond dispute. It was not the first time he wished he had studied biochemistry more thoroughly on his home world. He trusted contact with the check team could be made soon; they would certainly have specialists in this field among their numbers.

But he had to get back to work. He could clean up the ruined arm and expect it to be replaced, however slowly, by normal healing. The real worry was Bob's brain. Some of the bacteria as well as their toxins must have been carried to that organ by his circulatory system, and it could not be taken for granted that nothing had left the blood vessels to lodge in nerve tissue.

The Hunter had always been afraid to intrude into this material himself, though he had maintained a network of his own tissue in the capillaries. Brain cells were the objects where he was most afraid of making a mistake based on differences between human biochemistry and what he was more used to. Now it was necessary to take the chance, and he took it; but he worked very, very slowly and very, very carefully.

The situation was one he had never been able to explain at all clearly either to his host or to Seever, who had been curious about it. The Hunter did possess the ability to sense directly structures down to the large-molecule level. At the same time he could be aware simultaneously of the trillions of cells in a living organism, and work on them all at once with the same attention to each that a jeweler could give to a single watch. When he tried to describe this to a human being, however, it seemed to involve a contrast for his listener; the human seemed to think of him as a whole race of beings instead of an individual. This tended to bother the Hunter, because he could only think of himself as an individual.

Sometimes, facing problems which seemed beyond his ability, he wished there *were* more of him.

He did solve this one, for the time being. Relatively few bacteria had actually reached Bob's brain cells, and the alien managed to destroy these with comparatively little damage to nearby cells. He knew that these would not be repaired or replaced; it was the same with every humanoid species he knew, and was assumed by the scientists of his own kind to be an evolutionary byproduct of overspecialization of the brain cell. However, the brain itself was a highly redundant structure, and even though Bob was losing thousands of its cells every day, it would be many years before the cumulative effect became serious.

And at the moment, there was little point in worrying years ahead.

Bob was conscious and, except for the arm, normal by Monday night. He was still in the hospital section of the Seevers' home—Mrs. Seever remarked that with two patients, the place was more like a hospital than it had been for years—and after dinner the entire group assembled to bring everything up to date. Even Bob's parents were present; Daphne was spending the night with a friend.

The Hunter explained in detail what had happened to him, stressing the obvious fact that his people must be somewhere around, and mentioning as little as possible the lack of alertness which had led to such unfortunate results. The others told him of the message left at the ship, and its details, of which he approved. He agreed with the doctor that his entry into the ship had probably tripped a signal at the same time that it had released the paralyzing agent, so the check team was no doubt aware that the ship had been visited. What they would think when they found the small valve open but no prisoner on hand could only be guessed. Of course, if they found the message all would be well, but the Hunter agreed with Bob's pessimistic view that they had probably responded to the signal before the bottle had been placed. It would have been less surprising if they had arrived before the pipe containing his helpless form had been pulled up.

"They would be able to get to any place on Earth in an hour or so, and wouldn't have to wait until night to check out the ship," the Hunter assured his human friends.

"Then we'd better get back to it as soon as we can," Maeta responded. "We'll try, or the Hunter will try, to tell whether the bottle message has been found and read; but more important, we will leave a much more complete message in the Hunter's own language, with instructions on just where to meet him and how to recognize Bob. You didn't cover that in your note, did you, Bob?"

"No. I didn't think of it. I was more concerned with getting the history down. If they've read it, at least they'll know the other creature is dead, and there's no more need for booby traps."

"They'll have *heard,* if they read it, that the other one is dead. Will they believe it?" asked Seever.

"That's why the Hunter will have to supplement that message," Maeta pointed out. "He should be able to identify himself clearly in some way—a serial number, or something like that."

"But I put my name on my note," Bob said. "They should be able to find me."

"Why?" asked the dark-haired girl. "We can't take for granted that they know all about Ell and its people."

"Why not? They must have investigated the island pretty well when they first came. They'd probably have found us then, only I expect the Hunter and I weren't here."

"But why would they have known the people by name?" Maeta countered. "I suppose they'd have used human hosts the way the Hunter did, but they wouldn't have gotten in touch with them, would they? Talked to them, and used their help the way the Hunter used yours?"

"Definitely not," the detective said. "Unless some very special situation like mine demanded it, that would be extremely contrary to policy. I did it because I didn't at the time think there was the slightest chance of help from home, and my quarry was a danger to your people."

"Right," Maeta nodded. "And whoever is here, they haven't been hanging around Ell all these years just getting to know these particular people. For one thing, if they had, wouldn't we have more people on the island in Bob's condition? Hunter addicts, if you don't mind?"

"Very unlikely," the alien replied. "The group would have specialists able to forestall such events. That's why we're trying to get in touch with them, remember."

"But you should still add something of your own to Bob's message."

"He agrees," Bob relayed. "He says to get another bottle—a very small one will do—and something that will scratch glass. Do you have a carborundum scriber, or a small diamond, Doc?"

"I can get a scriber," Bob's father said.

"He doesn't want the whole tool, just the carbo tip. He's going to write on the inside of the bottle, and he probably couldn't maneuver the whole tool in there even if he could get it through the neck. He won't need a cork or sand ballast. He says he'll just tie the new bottle to the neck of the old one, to make something sure to attract attention."

"Then we can really count on being in touch with someone who can cure Bob, at last?" It was his mother, her voice not very steady. "It's been nice for those who could take this all as an intellectual problem, but I haven't been able to do that."

Bob answered his mother with a simple affirmative, but the Hunter's honesty forced him to go farther.

"If only police personnel like myself are on Earth, it may take longer. We might have to wait for a ship to go home and return with the specialist Bob needs."

"I don't want to mention that," Bob muttered back. "Why give her any more to worry about?"

"Don't be shortsightedly selfish," his symbiont admonished him. "If events disappoint her, you won't be in a position to care; but she has the right to reality. You know that."

"I know you, anyway." Reluctantly, Bob relayed the Hunter's qualification. His mother took a deep breath and shook her head. Then she looked at her son and said, "Thanks, Hunter." Bob raised his eyebrows. "And you, of course, Son."

That ended the discussion. Bob was falling asleep, and his parents and Maeta prepared to leave.

"When should I bring that carbide tip, Hunter?" Arthur Kinnaird asked as they reached the door. "Tonight? I can find one all right."

"No," Bob relayed. "He'll have to leave me to do that job, and says he won't do that before tomorrow night. You can all go back to normal living for a day. He'll do the message tomorrow night if I'm all right, and it can go out to the ship on Wednesday." His father nodded understanding, and Bob was asleep a minute later.

The Hunter spent the night as usual, going over and over his host's biochemistry in the endless effort to balance things better. The joint pains had been absent that day, leaving the alien to wonder whether the infection toxins, the inactivity, Seever's antibiotics, or even the symbiont's own absence might be responsible. He ended the night in his usual mood of futility and frustration.

Bob's arm progressed normally the next day, as did his other injuries. The heart muscle was essentially healed; it had been a clean wound, splitting muscle fibers more than tearing them. The Hunter no longer had to pay much attention to face and ear, though his host complained frequently of itching at both sites. The source of these nerve signals remained obscure to the detective, but he could not bring himself to make a major project of finding it.

Arthur brought the carbide tip during the afternoon, and Seever furnished a plain, thin-walled two-hundred-milliliter bottle; so during the night the Hunter was able to leave Bob for a few hours to write his message on the inner side of the glass. It was a harder job than he had expected. The carbide cut the glass readily enough, but a good deal of force had to be applied. He covered a quarter of the bottle's inner surface with script which would have been microscopic to a human being.

He tried to include all the information which might be necessary to convince the readers of his identity—clearly they weren't at all sure that his quarry wasn't around, too—and to let them find and identify at least one of the human members of the group. He also outlined his difficulty with his host's chemical machinery, making no effort to belittle his own mistakes in the matter. He had planned the wording carefully and, in spite of the unexpected difficulty, was back with his host in little over three hours.

Bob was able to rise without too much discomfort the next morning. The wind had been high the day before, causing everyone some uneasiness, and he insisted on accompanying Maeta to North Beach. They were alone; it was understood that if it was practical to go out, Maeta would bicycle back to get Bob's mother and Mrs. Seever.

The sun was well up when they reached North Beach, for Bob had slept fairly late. As they approached the outrigger, a small figure which had been seated beside it rose and faced them.

Once again the Hunter was impressed by André's plumpness, a rare condition among the Ell children. The generally accepted way of life among them involved intense activity, and Daphne, he remembered, liked to show off her very visible ribs. All three in the group were even more impressed by the thought of what might have happened to the outrigger before their arrival. However, Maeta greeted the child with her usual calm friendliness. She might have been about to ask, tactfully, what he was doing there, but he didn't give her the time.

"Can I go out with you?" the boy asked.

"Why?" retorted Bob.

"I want to see what you're doing. You have the Tavaké's metal-finder. I always wanted to try it and they'd never let me, and I've been wondering what metal you could be looking for outside the reef. No one ever drops tools there, and it wouldn't be worth looking for them if they did. Are you treasure-hunting?"

"No." Bob's tone was less cordial than was strictly tactful. "Why do you care what grown-ups are doing? Why don't you go with the other kids?"

"Them?" the youngster shrugged his shoulders. "They're no fun. I'd rather see what you're doing."

"We're not tripping bikes, or playing with their brakes or handlebars, or hiding glass in the sand," was Bob's even less tactful answer. André's face became more unexpressive than usual. Then he realized that this was hardly natural, and he put on the appearance of surprise. Then he realized that this had come too late, and gave another shrug.

"All right, forget it. I didn't think you'd want me. The kids you think I should be playing with don't, either. I'll think of something else." He turned away.

Neither the Hunter nor his host could quite decide how to respond to this bitter and pitiful remark, but Maeta did not hesitate.

"André, you're not making sense. If you really played the tricks Bob mentioned, wouldn't you expect people to be too afraid of you to want you around? And you did play them, didn't you?" The boy eyed her silently for fully a minute.

"Sure I did," he said at last, defiantly. "You know it. Jenny caught me out when she was talking to me the other day, and she told you."

"How do you know she told us?"

"I heard her. I listened outside the window after she went back to the other room with the rest of you."

Bob tried to conceal how this confession affected him. "What did you hear?" he asked.

"Lots."

Bob had never taken lessons from his guest detective, but even he knew better than to be specific.

"Have you listened before?"

"Sure. Lots."

"When have you listened to us?"

"In the hospital, mostly. Down by the creek, the day you and Jenny had been out on Apu, and she and your sister went to the library for the thing you were looking for. On the dock, the night you came back from the States."

"Did you try to break into my footlocker?"

"No. I was trying something else, that time. Your father said a lot, when he got hurt picking it up."

Maeta interjected. "Andy, do you snoop like this around everyone, or is there something about Bob and Jenny and me that interests you?"

"I listen whenever I can. If it's no fun, I stop. You've been a lot of fun."

"I can see where we might be," Bob said wryly. "What's been so especially fun about us for you?"

"The green things." The child's face was still inscrutable. "The green things that keep you from getting hurt. One of them kept your father from being burned up when I was little." That, the Hunter thought, was an interesting interpretation of the event; he wondered whether it had been edited. For the first time, he began to think there might be something to Seever's suspicion about his old quarry. André went on. "I wanted to get one for my father, because Mother had died. Then when the other kids used to hurt me, I wanted one for me."

"You thought, way back then, that there were green things that kept people from being hurt?" Bob was trying to be sure.

"Of course. I saw you with it at that fire. I wondered how you got one, and kept trying to find out who had them. I was never sure until the other day when I saw one come part way out of your hand while you were asleep up at the other end of the island. I walked with you for a way after that, and wanted to ask, but I

thought you wouldn't want to tell me. I just couldn't
really believe it, and I had to make sure. You didn't
get hurt, they told me, when you fell off your bike by
the library. I hadn't stayed, because I didn't think it
would work anyway—it was just an experiment. I
made real sure in your driveway."

"You certainly did," Bob admitted. He found himself at a loss for other words. Maeta, as usual, did not.

"Andy," she asked, "did you think what would have
happened if you'd been wrong about Bob and his—
green thing?"

"So I'd have been wrong. But I wasn't!" For the
first time there was an expression on the round face
—one of triumph. Bob and Maeta looked at each
other; then the girl turned back to the child.

"How about Jenny's foot?" she asked. "Did you
think she had one of them, too?"

"She might have. She had been with Bob, and they
were friends. He'd give one to a friend."

"And now you know she doesn't. Are you sorry?"

"She'll be all right." A thought crossed Bob's mind,
and he spoke up hastily.

"Before you try any more experiments, Andy,
Maeta doesn't have one. Neither does anyone else."

Maeta turned to the canoe. "You'd better come
along with us, André. You're only partly right about
all this, and we'll have to explain some things to you
before something really bad happens."

"Will you help me find one of them?"

"We're looking for them, but we can't give one to
you. They're people, and if you want one to live with
you you'll have to get him to like you. Come on. Bob's
arm is still bad from what you did, because his friend
can't fix broken bones any faster than they usually
heal. We were going to get someone else to help
paddle, but you'll do."

"I don't really want to go out with you. I know I
asked, but I didn't think you'd let me. The wind's too
high, and I'm afraid."

"We're taking an important message—really, really

important—to the green people. We may never find them if we don't get it there, where we think they'll be."

"Are they in the ocean?"

"Some of the time. Come along." The boy was still plainly reluctant, but Maeta had already displayed her force of personality, and the Hunter was not surprised when the youngster helped slide the outrigger into the water. Neither was Bob. Both of them, however, were uneasy about the girl's evident determination to go out with only two paddlers, one of them certainly not very strong and probably unskilled.

Since there was no way to ask her with the boy there—neither Bob nor the Hunter wanted to spoil any plan she might be considering—they could not know that Maeta had planned herself into a corner. She did want to get the bottle out to the spaceship; she regarded the message as vital to Bob's life. In addition, she, too, had suspected that André might have done something to her canoe, and wanted the assurance of seeing him afloat in it. Nothing less would convince her, for the moment, that he had played no tricks with the outrigger; and until they were actually afloat she was expecting him to come up with some last-minute excuse for staying behind.

The Hunter had thought along the same lines briefly, but had realized that if his enemy were actually in the boy and persuading him to do any of these tricks, it was perfectly possible that all the human beings on the canoe were likely to be drowned. The other creature would have no real interest in the welfare of its host, and would probably consider the child well spent in a maneuver which deprived the Hunter of his own host and an assistant. The aliens would not suffer as the canoe splintered against the reef. They would not drown; and things would be back where they were nearly eight years ago when the two representatives of the worst and the best of Castor's culture had reached Earth. Back where they were, except that this time the fugitive would be less likely to make any of the mistakes which had let the Hunter find him before.

The Hunter wondered what had been done to the canoe, and when it would make itself felt.

The wind, from the southwest, was still rising. Bob and his symbiont were getting more and more uneasy, and even Maeta was a little tense. She was beginning to wonder whether her judgment might not have suffered briefly from tunnel vision. She had stopped worrying about her canoe when they had reached deep water with André still aboard. Like both Bob and the Hunter in the last few weeks, she suddenly was feeling foolish; and, like the Hunter, she was worrying about what her mistakes might now do to other people.

In spite of the wind and her personal distraction, she found the marker buoy above the ship with surprising speed. It was still clear in spite of the wind, and the tanks in the lagoon which provided direction references were easy to see. She brought the canoe bow-on to the wind, and drew in her paddle.

"André, see if you can hold us here for a minute without my help. You can see that buoy; try to keep us just where we are with respect to it." The youngster, surprisingly to Bob, made no argument, but dug in with his paddle.

Bob was a little slow in reading the implications of Maeta's order, and by the time he turned to look at her she had slipped off the shirt and slacks which had covered her swimsuit, and was on her way overside with the bottle. Even the Hunter would have settled for dropping the message overboard at this point, and Bob was nearly frantic; but she gave no one time to expostulate. Bob got only part of a sentence out before she disappeared, leaving him quite literally holding his breath.

She was up again before he had to let it out, and slid aboard with her usual seallike grace. She snatched up her paddle, and snapped an order as she began to use it.

"Bob, be ready to lean out, or climb out, on the forward boom. I can't head straight for the beach, but even so the rigger will be upwind now. We're not a real double hull, and the outrigger is light; the wind may try to pick it up. Your job is not to let that happen. André, good work; keep paddling as you are."

It was much more difficult now. The wind had been more or less behind them on the way out; now it held them back. Maeta saw quickly that she was not allowing enough for drift, and pointed more to the west. She finally found a heading which seemed to offer a vector sum leading to the beach, but even André could see that it would be a long time getting them there. Maeta evidently decided it would take too long; after a few minutes she turned almost straight west, out to sea away from Ell.

"What's the idea?" Bob shouted over the wind.

"We can't make it back. André is wearing out, and I don't think I'll last that long myself. I want to get clear of the reef, and northwest is the quickest way. You can get off the boom, now."

"But we'll be blown out to sea!"

"I know. But Island Eight is about thirty-five miles away, and straight downwind as nearly as I can judge. We won't have much trouble hitting it—there's a compass here. We'll see it from miles away, and the tank there is unusually high, so if we miss the line a little we can still correct before we get there. Right now the important thing is to clear Ell's reef."

"And stay afloat."

Maeta gestured that qualification away with a toss of her head. She *knew* there was no worry from wind or wave on the open sea as long as she could manipulate a paddle. The confidence of competence was perhaps slightly inflated by the arrogance of youth, but she did know what she was doing. The error of putting to sea at all that day had been the result of attaching too much weight to factors unrelated to the weather;

she would, she still felt, do the same thing again as long as she could feel reasonably sure of delivering the message.

"How about the reef at Eight?" yelled Bob. "I've never been there."

"Neither have I," was the answer, "but Charlie says the passage is on this side and wide enough to be no problem—the tankers get in. Keep paddling just a little longer, Andy; you're doing fine."

She had gradually been heading more to the north as they drew away from Ell. Now, sure of her clearance, she bore around to the northeast and put the wind directly behind them. André was allowed to stop paddling, and Maeta herself eased off her efforts to what was necessary to hold their heading. They passed the northwest fringe of Ell's reef with two or three hundred yards to spare, though the breakers looked uncomfortably close to Bob.

Then there was empty sea before them. Maeta had estimated their speed, from the time it took to pass familiar objects along the northern reef, at about six knots—the wind, of course, was much higher, but had much less grip on the outrigger than the water did. This meant that the best part of six hours would be needed to reach Island Eight.

There was no danger of anyone's going to sleep. The canoe pitched violently enough to make it necessary to hold on most of the time, and spray blown from the tops of the waves made it necessary to bail fairly often. It was not, except for the first few minutes of doubt, a frightening trip even for the boy. None of them was really comfortable in the wind and spray, of course; Maeta put her slacks and shirt back on, soaked as they were, and André, who was clad only in shorts, forgot his independence and indifference enough to snuggle close to Bob for warmth. The Hunter thought of making a direct check for the presence of his not-certainly-dead quarry in the youngster's body, but could not be sure that it would be safe. If the boy moved very much, especially if he pulled away, while the alien was partly in one body and partly in the other, the results would be extremely unfortunate. The detective could of course afford to lose a few tiny tendrils, as he had at the ship, but such appendages might not be enough to find the other being. If the fugitive were actually there, he was aware of the Hunter's presence in Bob's body from the latter's recovery from the heart wound, and would be hiding—withdrawn into a single mass, or a few small masses, in body cavities, rather than spread out through the boy's system in a network ready for protective duty.

The Hunter mentioned all this to his host, and Bob agreed that unless the boy fell asleep the direct search would be unwise. André did not fall asleep.

By midafternoon, the tank of Island Eight was visible directly ahead. It was of experimental design, more than twice the usual twelve-to-fifteen-foot height of PFI's culture tanks, and visible from a much greater distance. Unfortunately, the experiment had not been very successful, and at the moment the unit was unused and the small atoll it occupied was uninhabited.

Half an hour after the first sighting, the breakers marking the reef became visible. At first, they stretched an equal distance to each side of the bow, with no sign of a break. Even Maeta was getting tense —it would soon be impossible to clear either side of the white water—when they finally sighted the passage, a little to their left. The girl altered their course slightly, and presently told André to start paddling again. Bob and the Hunter, neither able to do anything constructive, could only watch with increasing tension as the breakers drew closer. An occasional glance back at Maeta's face was somewhat reassuring, but not entirely; one could interpret her expression as one either of concentration or of worry.

The passage might, as Maeta's brother had said, be wide enough for a small tanker, but it looked awkwardly narrow at the moment. It was straight, the girl knew—it would have been made so for the tankers if it had not been that way naturally—but unfortunately it was not quite in the wind's direction. Once into it, they would have to paddle hard to the right to avoid being blown into the left side of the channel. Maeta, to give them as much room as possible for leeway, cut as closely as she dared to the breakers on the right as they entered.

The reef was low, and gave no protection at all from the wind. It broke the waves, but this was worse than useless; instead of coming harmlessly under their stern and lifting the canoe for a moment, the water now was hurled skyward by the coral and shredded into spray by the wind. As the outrigger made its turn into the passage, everyone aboard was blinded, and the canoe itself began to fill rapidly.

"Both of you bail!" cried Maeta. "I'll do the paddling!"

She could not see where they were going, and her only way to maintain heading was to keep the impact of the spray on the right side of her back. No one with only human senses and muscles could have done much better.

They emerged from the worst of the spray to find themselves almost on the coral that rimmed the left side of the passage. Maeta made a frantic effort to sweep them still more to the right, but simply wasn't strong enough. They very nearly made it, but struck unyielding coral only a yard or two from the relative safety of the lagoon.

The main hull of the canoe may have survived briefly, but the three human bodies were hurled forward. Bob struck André a split second before Maeta hurtled into both of them. There was another violent bump which they deduced later was the boy striking the bow of the canoe. The tangled bodies did a half somersault, found themselves either under water or in spray too dense to let them breathe, and felt one more violent shock. Then they were lying together on hard sand, spray still blowing over them.

Bob was conscious and not too badly hurt. The

Hunter had taken care, reflexively, of a number of small cuts from coral, but he had been cushioned to a large extent by the other two bodies. Neither of these was nearly as well off.

13. Reconstruction

André was unconscious, but had only minor visible cuts and scrapes. Though this would have been a good time to check for the presence of a symbiont, Bob paid little attention to him, because Maeta was in far worse condition. She had been underneath when they hit the coral. Deep cuts covered her back and hips, and much flesh had been torn from her right leg. Arterial blood was spurting over the sand, and being quickly diluted to invisibility by the spray.

Bob and his partner saw and evaluated the situation instantly, and reacted almost as promptly. The human member of the team grasped the injured leg just above the knee, pressed the heel of his hand against the most prominent source of bleeding, and snapped to his partner, "Get in there and earn your living! I'll hold on long enough to be sure you're there, but give me a twinge in the palm of the hand ten seconds or so before you're completely out of me."

The Hunter, just for a moment, thought of objecting on the grounds that Bob was his primary responsibility and was also injured. He even started to mention this, though he had already started the transfer and knew what Bob's answer would be. He was right.

"Stop dithering," snarled the young man. "None of

these nicks will let me bleed to death even if my clotting isn't up to par, and she'll be dead in five minutes if you don't take care of her. I can't hold all this bleeding; I haven't enough hands. I assume you've already taken care of any infecting organisms that got into me, and even if you haven't you can come back, or partly back, to do it later. And don't waste time going just through my hand—I know what you look like, and it's years too late to shock me. Hurry up!"

The alien obeyed, and within half a minute had the worst of the girl's bleeding stopped. It took four or five more to complete the transfer, partly because he found it difficult to pull himself away from the regions of Bob's injuries. It took a surprising effort to force intelligence to overcome habit; he was somewhat addicted to Bob, in a sense, too.

He was relieved, though quite surprised, to find that Maeta had no fractures, though several fragments of coral had broken off at the impact and were deeply imbedded in the injured leg. Her unconsciousness was due entirely to loss of blood, and he had to take rapid steps to counteract shock.

What she really needed most was replacement material—food. The easiest way to provide this would have been for the Hunter to catch and digest something, and release amino acids into her circulatory system. If there had been a dead fish or crab beside her it would have helped greatly. There wasn't, however, and with the wind and spray still lashing the islet on which they were stranded, there would be little chance for Bob to find anything even if he knew of the need.

Bob himself at the moment was more concerned with the small boy. He examined the limp form as carefully as possible, ascertained that at least none of the major limbs was fractured, and straightened him out into a more comfortable position. There was a little bleeding from relatively minor nicks and scrapes, but this was already stopping. Bob's was not, but he refused to worry about it yet. His broken arm seemed to be no worse than it had been.

While he was considering what to do, the shadow of the tank gradually extended across the islet. Even Bob, used to New England temperatures, felt a new chill in his wet clothes, and realized that something would have to be done for the night if the injured ones were not to die of exposure. Tropical Pacific water and tropical Pacific air are not very cold, but they are below human body temperature and can carry heat from a human body faster than that body can replace it.

For warmth, all Bob could think of was a hole in the sand. He scooped out one big enough for the three of them and covered them all, fairly completely, with more sand. This was wet with the spray, of course, but water did not move through it very fast; once it was warm, it stayed so. The combined heat loss of the three bodies dropped to a level their combined metabolisms—the Hunter's didn't count significantly—could offset.

The detective took advantage of the situation to send a pseudopod into Bob's ear and tell him about Maeta's real need for food. It was a slightly risky action, but he could have spared the tissue if Bob had moved inopportunely. He could probably, for that matter, have recovered it.

With much less danger he explored the unconscious André and established that there was no symbiont in the child's body; the boy was genuinely plump. He also had a broken collar bone which Bob had missed, but there was nothing the Hunter could do about this. Setting it was far beyond his strength.

The boy regained consciousness during the night. He was no longer self-possessed; he wept loudly and almost continuously, partly from pain and partly from terror. For the first time since the fire accident which Jenny had tried to use as a lesson, he was realizing that really serious things, not just minor pain that a "green thing" could take care of, could happen to *him*. Bob, wide awake because of his own discomfort, sympathized, yet he also hoped that the event would prove educational for André.

The night proved long even for the Hunter, who had plenty to keep him from boredom. It took several hours to work the fragments of coral out of Maeta's tissue without doing even more damage. He could do nothing to speed the formation of new blood cells or other tissue until food was available, but he held the torn flesh in position so that healing need not involve extensive bridges of scar tissue. As long as the young woman remained unconscious, nothing needed to be done about pain, and she was unlikely to wake up for many hours with so much blood gone. The alien was ready for it when it should happen, however.

He had some cause to feel useful. Without him she would have been dead in minutes from blood loss; or, failing that, from shock within an hour or two. If he could stay with her for a few days, she would not even be scarred, a factor which the girl herself would certainly appreciate and which, the Hunter had reason to suspect, would also be appreciated by his own host.

That left him free to worry about Bob, who must certainly have picked up more infecting microorganisms from the sand in his unclotted wounds. The Hunter had indeed disposed of the original ones, but recent experience had made it clear that it would not take long to get his partner back into serious trouble. The Hunter hoped he would not have to decide between Bob and Maeta. There was no question where his responsibility lay, but if he saved Bob and let the girl die, the former would be extremely hard to live with for a time.

The wind was much weaker by sunrise, and an hour later they were no longer being soaked by spray from the reef. Bob removed the sand cover to let the sun warm them, looked over his own scratches without saying anything to the Hunter, and bent to examine André. The boy had been quiet for some time, and the conscious members of the group had hoped that he was asleep, but he answered at once when Bob asked how he felt.

"Terrible," was the answer. "My shoulder hurts, and I'm cold and hungry."

"You'll probably be too warm when the sun gets a little higher. There's no shade here. We should be able to find some shellfish. I don't know what I can do about your shoulder; let me see."

The boy sat up, but shrank away the moment he was touched. "That hurts. Stop it."

"All right," Bob said. "I'm no doctor, anyway, and you didn't give me much chance to feel, but you'd better assume that something is broken in there, and keep it still." The Hunter had not reported to Bob on the boy's condition. "Does it hurt to move your arm?"

"Yes. A lot."

"Then let's get my shirt off and let me try to make it into a sling for you, so the arm won't move. You'll have to decide whether you want to put up with the pain while I do that, so there'll be less pain later, or not. I'm not going to waste time arguing."

"Leave it alone. Why can't your green thing help me?"

"He's busy with Maeta, who needs him a lot worse than you do." The boy looked at Maeta closely for the first time, turned visibly pale, and said nothing for several seconds. Then he looked at his own shoulder, which was by now covered with a single huge area of blue, black, and yellow bruise. He seemed about to say something, looked back at Maeta's torn back and leg, and walked away down the beach.

"Find some shellfish!" Bob called after him. There was no answer.

"I'll find something for you and Mae, Hunter," Bob said, giving up André as a minor problem for the moment. "Stand by a couple of minutes. There'll surely be something around, since you're not choosy. I'll have to work fast; these cuts of mine are starting to hurt a lot, and I may have to stay put in a little while and let you work on both of us, if you possibly can."

The Hunter had no way of answering. He thought intensely as he watched Bob walk off after the boy, through the temporary eye he had improvised. It might have been better for Bob to go in the opposite direction, but there was no opposite direction to go; they were at the end of a small island immediately beside the reef passage. The two or three hundred yards of sand to the northwest, merging into coral on the side toward the breakers, were their total resource area. There were other islets around the atoll, and the culture tank occupied most of the tiny lagoon, but the canoe was gone. Two of them could not possibly swim, and Bob was not likely to take the risk in his present condition. It might be impossible for him, too, in a few hours.

The Hunter decided to waste a little of Maeta's blood, and began to permit clots to form over her injuries. She might have to hold the rest of it in by herself for a while.

Bob was back in a minute or two with a large fish which seemed to have been washed through the reef and stranded. It was in very unappetizing condition for a human being, but quite usable for the Hunter. He set it down beside the still unconscious girl; the alien extruded tissue from her skin, enveloped the fish, and began salvaging amino acids and carbohydrates. It massed ten or twelve pounds, quite enough for immediate needs. The Hunter concentrated on his job, but tried to keep aware of the other two.

They found enough food to keep them going, though Bob was not at all fond of shellfish; but as the day wore on, the far more serious question of water began to loom.

There was no spring or rivulet on the little island. The few pools which existed had been filled by the spray, and were rapidly vanishing in any case. Bob considered complaining to be beneath him, but the child did not, and his whines about his thirst alternated with questions about when they could expect to be rescued.

Bob was optimistic about this. "They know we were out in Mae's canoe, or they could have found out soon enough when we didn't show up for supper. They'd know which way the wind would send us. The Dumbo was at Tahiti, but they'd call it down by radio this morning, and this island will be about the first place they'll look. If you want to be useful instead of noisey, go and make a great big "S O S" on the beach—as big as you can fit between the coral and the lagoon. I expect they'll see us easily enough anyway, since there's nothing to hide us, but that would catch an eye from farther away."

The Hunter took Bob's words at their face value, since they seemed reasonable, and stopped worrying about water as far as the males were concerned; they could last for a day or so. Maeta, however, could not; she had lost far too much blood. She regained consciousness about noon, and the symbiont explained the situation to her, vibrating her hearing apparatus as he normally did Bob's. She took it calmly enough, but her first words were also about water. The Hunter admitted that none was available.

"Are you sure you can't do anything about that?" she asked. "I don't want to sound like a crybaby, but I don't know all about your powers. I know you can do funny things with body chemistry, and I wondered if you could take the salt out of sea water if I drank it, or maybe filter it out of the water before it got into us? Or could a person dip an arm or a leg into the sea, and have you bring in just water through the skin and leave the salt outside?"

The Hunter admitted that this might be possible; there were organisms on his world which possessed desalting organs, though he knew only in a very general way how these worked.

"It will certainly take energy," the detective pointed out. "It's a pity that you, who need the water most because of your blood loss, have such a poor food reserve. I did feed you a lot from the fish Bob brought, but most of it's already gone to repair and reconstruction. I'm not really sure I can do this desalting trick, since I've never had to do it before, but I'll try. Ask Bob to get you into the water."

"Even if you can't do it," she said, "it will be more comfortable there. It's pretty hot here on the sand. I remember long ago when I was working out on one of the reef islets at Ell, and the people who were supposed to pick me up were late, I felt a lot better just lying in the water while I waited. Maybe a person's skin can take water out of the ocean anyway."

The Hunter assured her that it could not—that water would normally tend to flow the other way, if at all, osmosis being what it was. To his surprise, she knew what he was talking about, and conceded the point, theoretically.

"But then I should have gotten thirstier that day, and not felt better," she remarked. The Hunter, willing to prolong any discussion to keep the girl's mind off her very genuine thirst, pointed out that the human species seemed to him a very suggestible one. She did not answer this; Bob had approached, and she was telling him what the Hunter had said about getting her into the water. Bob, of course, knew the osmosis situation equally well and rather doubted the practicality of the attempt, but decided not to argue with the Hunter. The water, fortunately, was only a few feet away, and with a little help from the girl herself he got her legs and feet immersed as much as the very shallow slope of the beach allowed. The Hunter sent out his own tissue through her skin, and tried to remember what he had learned about desalting glands.

It was a difficult job. His chemical senses operated essentially on large molecules such as proteins and polysaccharides; he could identify and distinguish these by means most nearly analogous to the human sense of touch. It was intuitively obvious to him why many of them behaved as they did in a human organism—or any other living thing—just as a simple gear train is obvious in its operation to most human beings. However, if the same human being, who had no training in complex mechanics, were suddenly to be confronted with the maintenance of a twenty-eight cylinder "corncob" airplane engine, he would be in somewhat the Hunter's situation faced with the upkeep of a living body from a planet his people had not visited before.

The salt problem looked simpler, but actually branched out into another field. It was a little like asking a mechanic who had been trained on the airplane engine to work on a television set. The sodium and chloride ions, as well as the magnesium and other chemical species in sea water, were very different from proteins—far smaller, and too uniformly charged to offer a handle to most of the alien's sensing and manipulating powers. He knew that all living cells had selective permeability to such things by nature of their chemical architecture. He knew some of the ways in which this was done, but by no means all of them; even to him, a cell was a very complex structure. On a scale which represents a water molecule by a fairly large pea, a human red blood cell is over half a mile across, and has much detail to be learned by anyone proposing to repair or alter its structure—or even imitate it.

There were many members of the Hunter's species to whom the construction of an effective desalting gland would have been a trivial matter, but the highly experienced detective was not among them.

He tried, but asking Maeta occasionally how she felt was superfluous. He knew that he was getting very little deionized water through her skin.

Bob kept feeding them, and of course a certain amount of water was available from the oxidized foods, but it was not enough to keep the girl comfortable. The Hunter could, and did, block the nerves which would have been transmitting excruciating pain from her injuries, but the thirst sensation was far

more subtle in origin, and he could do nothing about
it.

Maeta did not complain, but sometimes she could
not help saying something which showed how she felt.
She never blamed the Hunter or anyone else, except
once to comment on her own poor judgment in putting
to sea when she had. But to the detective the whole
situation was obviously his own fault. His feelings of
guilt never wavered. He wished she would not talk at
all, but could not bring himself to ask her not to.

It was fortunate that he did not. It was one of her
remarks which dropped the most important piece of
the jigsaw puzzle into place for him. The remark was
painful to him, painful enough so that he could not
resist arguing, in fact, but it proved useful.

"I'm afraid I felt better the other time I fought
thirst this way, Hunter," she said. "I suppose it isn't
working so well this time because I've been hurt so.
You're sure I won't die of thirst this time?"

"Unless it takes two or three days for us to be
found," the symbiont assured her, "you're in no real
danger. With enough food, I could get the water to
keep you alive indefinitely, though perhaps not very
comfortably. I'm getting a little into you from the sea,
too—more than would come through your skin without help, in spite of what you were saying."

"That's hard to believe," she said slowly and drow-
sily. "The other time I didn't get thirsty at all. I remember." The Hunter was slightly irritated by his
failure at what the human beings considered a simple
job. His answer showed this slightly.

"It may have been your additional reserves, Maeta,
but I suspect it's just ordinary human good-old-times
reaction," he said. "There is just no way that signifi-
cant amounts of water—even sea water—could get
through your skin, which is effectively designed to keep
water inside your system. If any did get in, it wouldn't
help your thirst at all."

"It did. I remember. Twice."

"But you weren't hurt, and you were only a few

hours without water, and you knew it was coming soon. You've never been in a situation like this, I'm sure."

"I wasn't hurt, no, and the first time, you're right—it was only five or six hours and I'd emptied my canteen without thinking how long I was going to be there. I was a little careless in those days. The second time I'd accidentally spilled my bucket during the first hour, and I'd done a lot of work and was really thirsty before I noticed it had tipped. The boat didn't come back to pick me up until way after dark. It was a very long day. And I soaked in the lagoon. And I didn't get thirsty."

A thought crossed the Hunter's mind, startling enough to silence him for several seconds while he tried to work out its implications.

Finally he asked, "How long ago was all this? The last two or three years, or back when you were very young?"

Maeta answered with no hesitation. "Not very long ago. Both times, I was collecting for the Museum Exchange—that's the group that arranges trades of specimens between exhibitors and collectors all over the world—and I didn't start working with them until after I started at the library, of course. I didn't know about them until then."

"Less than three years, then."

"About that," she agreed.

The Hunter decided not to ask for details about the carelessness she had been showing at about that time. She was a very alert young woman, he had come to realize, and he did not want her thinking, just yet, along the lines which had just occurred to him. He was not sure enough yet; one didn't jump to conclusions, at least not out loud.

Also, he didn't know whether to be annoyed at the waste of the time spent on looking for spaceships, or to be relieved that there would be no need to deliver any more messages to the one with the booby trap.

14. Professional

The amphibian settled onto Eight's lagoon about an hour before sunset, and taxied close to the beach where the castaways were waiting. A rubber dinghy emerged from the waist hatch, followed by Dr. Seever. He paddled ashore without waiting for anyone to accompany him, and looked over the three standing and lying at the water's edge. He whistled gently as he saw Maeta.

"Ladies first, it looks like," he remarked as he stepped out of the dinghy and pulled it ashore. He started to bend down for a closer examination, and was visibly startled at the cheerful way the girl spoke.

"I'm reasonably all right, Doctor," she said. "The Hunter is with me, and all I need is a gallon or so of water. Better check up on Bob; he got some cuts when we landed."

"I'll last," Bob forestalled questioning. "I was getting feverish two or three hours ago, and Mae noticed it. She told the Hunter to come over and clean me out. I objected, but you don't argue with her, as you may have noticed. She had the Hunter on her side, anyway. He took care of the bugs and went back to her, so I'm all right for a while."

"And how about me?" asked André.

"A broken shoulder, I think," Bob said to the doctor. "He may look the best, if you don't count that bruise, but he probably does need you the most."

Seever sighed. "Hunter, if your people really decide to make close contact with humanity, medical practice is certainly going to change a lot. I suppose I should be grateful that it won't disappear entirely, though maybe I wouldn't mind retiring early at that. Come on, all of you. I'll work on you in the plane, Andy. I gather you've joined the group."

"Well," said Bob, "we have to do something to keep him from sticking skewers through people just to see if they can live through it. Maybe you should train him as a surgical assistant, Doc."

By the time the amphibian reached Ell, Seever had immobilized the broken shoulder, used human remedies on Bob's contusions, and dressed Maeta's injuries for the sake of appearances. The Hunter was impatient to get back, since he did not want to discuss his new conclusions in front of André, who could be counted on to contribute to the violation of several regulations if he heard them. The boy had been convinced for the moment that he should keep word of the "green things" to himself by stressing the earlier argument—that they didn't want the word to get around, and would be unlikely to form friendships with anyone who let out their secret. It was obvious that more steps were going to have to be taken, but no one knew just what they would be.

The main thing was to get a Castorian professional xenobiologist to work on Bob, and the Hunter wanted to get back to Ell for that purpose. He had finally decided which were the key data, and fitted them together into a coherent picture—the moving generator shield, the booby-trapped spaceship, the fact that the fugitive's ship was in so much better shape than his own had been, the room in the library with the large armchair, the library itself, Maeta's session of carelessness and her experience in fighting thirst with a dip in the sea, and the results of his own staying with Bob for over seven years. He was sure that police procedure meant little now, since the Castorian police had left long before. What he needed was the headquarters of the team which was evaluating Earth and humanity.

And it was quite obvious where they were. There remained just the small, practical problem of getting in touch with a group of scientists who had been warned that a dangerous criminal might still be loose on Earth, without being killed by them. The messages at the ship were useless; the scientists might possibly visit it once a year, if they felt they could spare the time. Another message had to be delivered, but not to the ship. The place was obvious now, and the Hunter was angry with himself for not thinking of it earlier. The method of delivery was almost as obvious, but the Hunter rather hoped that his human colleagues would make themselves look as foolish as he himself had done. He was quite frank about this, when the entire in-group except André were gathered in Maeta's hospital room the night of their rescue from Eight. The girl had quickly mastered the art of relaying what he said to her, without having to pause to listen to him, and the exposition went smoothly.

"First," he started with a question, "is young André safely asleep? He's displayed more skill than I like at hearing what isn't meant for him."

"He's in the next room, but sound asleep," Seever replied. "He was uncomfortable enough to accept medication."

"And you're absolutely sure he took it?"

"Yes. I watched him drink it, made sure it wasn't spilled anywhere, and had him talk to me afterward to be sure his mouth was empty. I'm learning, old as I am."

"All right," Maeta relayed. "I am now quite sure I know where to get in touch with the evaluation team from my home world, and we should be able to do it tomorrow. I feel very silly at not seeing it before, and wasting so much of everyone's time and effort, not to mention extending the danger to Bob's life and bringing danger to Jenny and Mae. I want to go through my detailed idea of what has happened on Ell during the last seven years, not because I feel the need for drama but because if I can get through the account without any of you seeing where my people must be, I won't have to feel so foolish. Several mystery novels which

Bob had read suggested the technique to me; forgive me if the suspense makes any of you uncomfortable.

"When we disposed of my original quarry—and it seems that we really did dispose of him, Doctor, and though absolute proof would be hard to supply, I examined André carefully—I was convinced that I was hopelessly lost from my own people. I had an unrealistic idea of the number of stars in the volume of space whose radius I had traversed. I don't blame myself greatly; a view of the star clouds of the Milky Way is extremely deceptive. Look at a photograph in any of your popular astronomy books; you will certainly not realize that a fair model of this part of the galaxy could be made by scattering tennis balls with an average separation of a thousand miles.

"After Bob and I had taken an astronomy course while he was in college, I realized that it should actually be quite simple for my people to trace us, and that a search had most probably been conducted. I am now quite sure that one of our ships reached Earth some time before March, 1949—your data, Mae—within fifteen months after we disposed of my quarry. They detected his ship, but not mine, probably because mine was far more badly damaged, and sea water had reached and corroded the units whose force fields are normally detectable from a distance. They investigated his ship, identified it, explored his possible paths to Ell, and found the generator case on Apu just as we had earlier. They had, after all, the advantage of knowing that such an object was missing from his ship, and must have looked for it specifically.

"Not finding any trace of me or my ship, they assumed that I had either failed to reach Earth at all, or had been killed by the crash, by Earth life, or by my quarry. It is also possible that they did find my ship, and deduced from its condition that I had never reached shore."

"But how could you have been killed by the crash?" asked Mrs. Kinnaird. "As I understand it, your ship was merely flattened, not burned or exploded. Merely mashing you up wouldn't kill you."

"You exaggerate a little," replied the Hunter, "but what probably would have killed me was the marine life. I told Bob and Jenny about my troubles while I was down in the pipe. If I hadn't met that shark, I might very well not have survived to reach Ell and find Bob." The woman nodded understandingly, and the alien went on. "In any case, my friends assumed that I was out of the picture, and that my quarry was loose somewhere on Earth—they hoped, but could not be sure, on Ell.

"Naturally they didn't find him. I suppose it's lucky they didn't find me, under the circumstances, though I might possibly have been able to identify myself to them in time. Anyway, they concluded the unsuccessful search, booby-trapped my quarry's ship, and went back home. Their report caused an evaluation team to be assembled and sent here. They arrived over three years ago—again from your data, Mae."

"I don't see that," the girl said, interrupting her own translation.

"I'm delighted. You will. I skipped one point; sorry. The police would have been the ones to move the generator shield, partly to experiment with it, to see why our quarry might have left it where he did, partly to prevent him from using it again too easily—he might, for all they could know, have been wandering around on Apu at the time. One of them would have stayed with it, probably armed with a paralyzer, in case the other did find it; but what happened was Maeta's picking it up."

"You mean one of your people was inside that thing when I took it home?" Maeta exclaimed.

"I'd be glad to bet any reasonable sum you like; and considering the date you found it, I'm sure it was one of the police group, not the later arrivals. You didn't look inside, I take it."

"Not carefully. It seemed to be full of sand, and I

left it outdoors to dry out before I took it into the house."

"Exactly. Into your house. One of your family, probably you, became host for a time to that policeman."

"But he never tried to talk to me!"

"Of course not. No emergency. He didn't find himself isolated halfway around your planet at his first chance to look through your eyes, as I did." The Hunter addressed the entire group again.

"I doubt that he stayed with Mae very long; he'd have wanted to move around a lot in his investigation. There must be a lot of ex-hosts around Ell at the moment.

"The next group eventually came, and started where the police had left off. They probably paid little if any attention to the booby-trapped ship. I'm sorry about that, as I said; it was a reasonable theory originally, but general procedures have to be modified by specific situations. My mistake was in taking too long to see how the specific situations applied. Anyway, the evaluation team came, and is here now. They're doing a job likely to take five or ten of your years. If the police reported human beings to be as different as they should have, there are probably fifty or so members of the team—including several of the specialists we need to get Bob back together. We'll take a note to their headquarters tomorrow."

"Where's that?" asked Jenny.

"I'll go along with your game, Hunter," said Maeta. "You implied that I'd served as a host another time. Is that relevant to your Agatha Christie puzzle? Bob, did you ever *feel* this creature *grinning?*"

"Can't say that I did," was the answer. "Let him go on."

The detective continued. "It is very relevant. I expect one of you to come up with the answer at any moment. Yes, Maeta, you were a host, probably several times. I suppose they shifted hosts often to avoid doing what I did to Bob—as I should have done, I see now. At least once, you had an expert who could manipulate the desalting operation; you were quite right, you really didn't get thirsty that time you were stranded on the reef."

"But why would they use me several times? There are a couple of hundred people on Ell—at least a hundred and fifty even if a lot of the children are too small."

"A strong and healthy host is very desirable; spending all our time in protection and repair is hardly life. We like to do things of our own, and the evaluation team members would have a great deal to do. Much more to the point, Mae," the girl continued to translate in spite of the personal nature of the next sentences, "you are one of the most conveniently located and occupied people on this island, for any member of the headquarters group of the evaluation team. Think, Miss Teroa. A place where an enormous volume of information about Earth and its people is stored in organized form. A place where a host can conveniently be made to feel sleepy if the symbiont wants to work alone for a time, and where a human being can unobtrusively be anesthetized briefly without risking his falling and hurting himself, if one of the team needs to spend a while with a host. You told Bob it was a very comfortable chair."

Maeta had not yet achieved Bob's skill at communicating with the Hunter without speaking aloud, but she tried.

"That last gives Bob and me an unfair advantage, don't you think? I see it now. Should I speak up?"

"Bob hasn't. Go ahead." The girl nodded, and spoke aloud.

"All right. Doctor, if you can lend me a crutch, I'll go to work tomorrow. There's still plenty to be done downstairs. If the Hunter will write a note in his own language tonight, I'll tuck it into that chair that Old Toke found too comfortable; and some time during the morning I'll take a rest in it. Maybe a larger sign that I can prop up on the table, so it can be read from the sides of the room, calling attention to the note in the chair, would also be a good idea. If I hear anyone coming, I can slip it under a book, so there won't be any violation of the rules. All right, Hunter?"

It was quite all right.

15. Official, from Headquarters

The Hunter's principal trouble, though not his only one, during the next several months stemmed from the personality of the specialist who took over Bob. This being was an intolerant and tactless individual who attached much weight to professional competence, had a high—fortunately justified—opinion of his own abilities, and failed completely to see how the detective could have been so stupid as to remain with a single host of a new species for such a long time. Since the Hunter had no excuse and had already been blaming himself for the slip, his own self-esteem was not healing at all rapidly. The fact that Bob disliked his new symbiont, made no bones about saying so, and openly looked forward to the time when he could have the Hunter back was some comfort to the latter, but not very much. Fortunately this attitude made no difference to the specialist, who regarded the young man as an interesting specimen, not a personal friend. The closest he came to approving of anything the Hunter had done made this more than clear.

The two were in direct contact, a situation which permitted their multi-purpose "cells" to act as nerves and transmit information between them at speeds far greater than oral speech could manage. The Hunter was in the library chair; Bob was seated there to permit the communication, carefully keeping his hands motionless on the stuffed arms.

"I must admit," the xenobiologist said, "that there has been one good result of your stupidity. I have been able to find out more about this species in a few months, from the various things you did to this being, than I could have ascertained from several years of legal experimentation. It is quite possible that in two or three more years I will be able to resolve the techniques which will allow us to live full time with these beings."

"Then Bob is going to be all right? You expect to be able to study him for years?"

"Of course. Isn't that what I implied? You are allowing yourself to be distracted from straightforward joint thinking."

"Why didn't you tell me sooner?"

"It was not important," said Xeno, as Bob had named him.

"It was to me," returned the Hunter. "You sound like one of those unreal scientists in the stories Bob reads. Do you know what a friend is?"

"Certainly. I have a number of friends myself; but your forming a close attachment to a member of this species was rather premature. In any case, it will be several years before I can allow you to resume symbiosis with this one. If you plan to remain on Earth, you should start living with other human beings. I can permit you to practice, but you are not to remain with any individual for more than half of one of their years. I suppose you will want to confine yourself to those who, as a result of your incompetence, already know about us."

"It would be a lot better than living in this library, even if the food does come regularly now—you'll have to admit that's an improvement on silverfish and the crumbs from librarians' lunches."

"It is more convenient, I grant. I trust you are not developing this highly subjective attitude human beings call *taste,* however. Food is fuel; as long as the quantity is sufficient, there is no reason to complain."

The Hunter broke contact, Xeno informed Bob that the conversation was over—the alien had learned English in connection with his evaluation work in the library—and the detective had no contact with the specialist for several days.

He spent some of the time with Maeta, whose injuries were completely healed, and reported Xeno's words to her.

"Then Bob is really going to be all right?" she asked. "He's looked so much happier, and doesn't have the fatigue or the joint pains any more, but I couldn't be sure that Xeno had really gotten to the cause of things."

"He knew that from the beginning," the Hunter admitted. "The problem was that I'd done so much damage that there was no certainty for a long time that it could be repaired. I thought I'd admitted that to you."

"You did," conceded the girl, "but I was hoping you'd forgotten. You were feeling pretty awful about the whole thing, and it wasn't really your fault. You couldn't have done anything else."

"Not at first," the alien admitted, "but later on I should have swapped around to other hosts. There were Bob's parents, and the doctor, who knew about me."

"Would you need that many? Wouldn't just back and forth between two people be all right?"

"I'd think so, but I'm not sure. I could ask Xeno. But isn't it rather academic now, anyway?"

"Not entirely," Maeta said. "You find out—and make sure when that cold-blooded molecule manipulator is going to be through with Bob, while you're at it. I think I can hold hands with him long enough for you two to get that much of a message across. Now think over those lessons in biochem that Xeno ordered you to memorize; I have book work to do."

About the Author

Hal Clement (Harry Clement Stubbs) was born in Massachusetts in 1922. He has been a science lover from early childhood, at least partly as a result of a 1930 *Buck Rogers* panel in which villains were "headed for Mars, forty-seven million miles away." His father, an accountant, couldn't answer the resulting questions, and led little Hal to the local library. The result was irreversible brain influence.

He majored in astronomy at Harvard, and has since acquired master's degrees in education and in chemistry. He earns his basic living as a teacher of chemistry and astronomy at Milton Academy, in Massachusetts, and regards science-fiction writing and painting as hobbies. His first two stories, "Proof" and "Impediment," were sold when he was a junior in college; their impression on Harvard's $400 yearly tuition secured family tolerance for that crazy Buck Rogers stuff.

He has since produced half a dozen novels, of which the best known are *Needle* and *Mission of Gravity*. His reputation among science-fiction enthusiasts is that of a "hard" writer—one who tries to stick faithfully to the physical sciences as they are currently understood; like Arthur C. Clarke and the late Willy Ley, Clement would never dream of having a space ship fall into the sun merely because its engines broke down. He can do his own orbit computing, and does.

He leads a double life, appearing frequently at science fiction conventions as Hal Clement and spending the rest of his time in Milton as Harry Stubbs, the rather square science teacher with a wife of twenty-five years and three grown children. He does occasional merit badge counselling for the Boy Scouts, has served on his town's finance committee, and is an eleven-gallon Red Cross blood donor.

NEW FROM BALLANTINE!

FALCONER, John Cheever   27300 $2.25

The unforgettable story of a substantial, middle-class man and the passions that propel him into murder, prison, and an undreamed-of liberation. "CHEEVER'S TRIUMPH . . . A GREAT AMERICAN NOVEL."—*Newsweek*

GOODBYE, W. H. Manville   27118 $2.25

What happens when a woman turns a sexual fantasy into a fatal reality? The erotic thriller of the year! "Powerful."—*Village Voice.* "Hypnotic."—*Cosmopolitan.*

**THE CAMERA NEVER BLINKS, Dan Rather
with Mickey Herskowitz**   27423 $2.25

In this candid book, the co-editor of "60 Minutes" sketches vivid portraits of numerous personalities including JFK, LBJ and Nixon, and discusses his famous colleagues.

THE DRAGONS OF EDEN, Carl Sagan 26031 $2.25

An exciting and witty exploration of mankind's intelligence from pre-recorded time to the fantasy of a future race, by America's most appealing scientific spokesman.

VALENTINA, Fern Michaels   26011 $1.95

Sold into slavery in the Third Crusade, Valentina becomes a queen, only to find herself a slave to love.

**THE BLACK DEATH, Gwyneth Cravens
and John S. Marr**   27155 $2.50

A totally plausible novel of the panic that strikes when the bubonic plague devastates New York.

**THE FLOWER OF THE STORM,
Beatrice Coogan**   27368 $2.50

Love, pride and high drama set against the turbulent background of 19th century Ireland as a beautiful young woman fights for her inheritance and the man she loves.

**THE JUDGMENT OF DEKE HUNTER,
George V. Higgins**   25862 $1.95

Tough, dirty, shrewd, telling! "The best novel Higgins has written. Deke Hunter should have as many friends as Eddie Coyle."—*Kirkus Reviews*

VERY FIRST AID

Bob gave a startled yell as he fell, but that was all his reflexes accomplished. The Hunter had provided the usual tightening up around the joints to help sprain defense. But neither reaction was really helpful.

Both forearm bones snapped; the flesh on Bob's left cheek was badly torn. But the Hunter didn't have to anesthetize him; the impact had knocked him out.

The alien had started repair work at once, preventing practically all blood loss, pulling displaced tissue back into its approximately correct place, when he heard steps. He assumed whoever was coming would instantly give help or go for it.

But he was wrong.

Suddenly a thin sliver of metal was plunged through his host's chest . . . and the Hunter realized immediately that his real work had just begun . . .